T0154511

DARK SATELLITES

Clemens Meyer was born in 1977 in Halle and lives in Leipzig. After high school he jobbed as a watchman, building worker and removal man. He studied creative writing at the German Literary Institute, Leipzig and was granted a scholarship by the Saxon Ministry of Science and Arts in 2002. His first novel, *Als wir träumten*, was a huge success and for his second book, *Die Nacht, die Lichter*, a collection of short stories, he was awarded the Leipzig Book Fair Prize 2008. *Bricks and Mortar*, his latest novel, was longlisted for the 2017 International Booker Prize and shortlisted for the 2019 Best Translated Book Awards.

Katy Derbyshire, originally from London, has lived in Berlin for over twenty years. She translates contemporary German writers including Inka Parei, Heike Geissler, Olga Grjasnowa, Annett Gröschner and Christa Wolf. Her translation of Clemens Meyer's *Bricks and Mortar* was the winner of the 2018 Straelener Übersetzerpreis (Straelen Prize for Translation). She occasionally teaches translation and also co-hosts a monthly translation lab and the bi-monthly Dead Ladies Show.

'Clemens Meyer's great art of describing people takes the form of the Russian doll principle: a story within a story within a story. From German jihad to a Prussian refugee drama, so much is so artfully interwoven that his work breaks the mould of the closed narrative. Images of history extending into the present are what make this collection a literary sensation.'
—— Katharina Teutsch, *Die Zeit*

'Dark Satellites proves once again that he is one of the strongest German writers. His short stories possess depth and truth, linking East German history with the present and painting dense and perceptive portraits of what we call 'common people' – without a trace of mawkishness or kitsch.'
—— Heinrich Oemsen, *Hamburger Abendblatt*

'Meyer's writing is brittle, laconic, clear, intense – and once again on top form. Short stories are clearly his forte. He finds memorable images for his themes: a dance without music in an unused Russian canteen; a midnight haircut; a man who slides into another identity after a break-in to his home and leaves his briefcase, the last requisite of his old life, in an abandoned shop. Meyer's stories are quiet, tragic and once again populated by ordinary people, for whom he has always harboured sympathies.'
—— Steffen Roye, *Am Erker*

Praise for *Bricks and Mortar*

'Meyer's multifaceted prose, studded with allusions to both high and popular culture, and superbly translated by Katy Derbyshire, is musical and often lyrical, elevating lowbrow punning and porn-speak into literary devices
... [*Bricks and Mortar*] is admirably ambitious and in many

places brilliant – a book that not only adapts an arsenal of modernist techniques for the twenty-first century but, more importantly, reveals their enduring poetic potential.'
— Anna Katharina Schaffner, *Times Literary Supplement*

'[*Bricks and Mortar* is a] stylistic tour de force about the sex trade in Germany from just before the demise of the old GDR to the present, as told through a chorus of voices and lucidly mangled musings. The result is a gripping narrative best described as organic.'
— Eileen Battersby, *Irish Times*

'A journey to the end of the night for 20/21st century Germany. Meyer reworks Döblin and Céline into a modern epic prose film with endless tracking shots of the gash of urban life, bought flesh and the financial transaction (the business of sex); memory as unspooling corrupted tape; journeys as migrations, as random as history and its splittings. A shimmering cast threatens to fly from the page, leaving only a revenant's dream – sky, weather, lights-on-nobody-home, buried bodies, night rain. What new prose should be and rarely is; Meyer rewrites the rules to produce a great hallucinatory channel-surfer of a novel.'
— Chris Petit, author of *Robinson*

'This is a wonderfully insightful, frank, exciting and heart-breaking read. Bricks and Mortar is like diving into a Force 10 gale of reality, full of strange voices, terrible events and a vision of neoliberal capitalism that is chillingly accurate.'
— A. L. Kennedy, author of *Serious Sweet*

'The point of *Im Stein* [*Bricks and Mortar*] is that nothing's "in stone": Clemens Meyer's novel reads like a shifty, corrupted collocation of .docs, lifted off the laptop of a master genre-ist and self-reviser. It's required reading for

fans of the Great Wolfgangs (Hilbig and Koeppen), and anyone interested in casual gunplay, drug use, or sex.'
—— Joshua Cohen, author of *Book of Numbers*

'The language is dizzying at times, frank and colloquial in others, but through Katy Derbyshire's glorious and award-winning translation, the reader is guided around this intoxicating, unflinching underworld without getting lost. Some of the content in *Bricks and Mortar* will be shocking to many, but this sombre drift through lonely nights and clandestine activities offers a fascinating and compelling take on post-Cold War Germany.'
—— Reece Choules, *The Culture Trip*

Praise for *All the Lights*

'His is a voice that demands attention, unafraid to do different, sometimes seemingly wrong-headed, things, confident in its ability to move, confront and engage his readers.'
—— Stuart Evers, author of *Your Father Sends His Love*

Fitzcarraldo Editions

DARK SATELLITES

CLEMENS MEYER

Translated by
KATY DERBYSHIRE

CONTENTS

ONE

We were working on an overgrown stretch of land next to a petrol station, right by a dual carriageway. It was hot and there were only a few trees for shade. The grass came up to our waists and we mowed it with strimmers, cutting off the little bushes just above the ground as well. We had spades and other tools with us for pulling up the roots. Someone wanted to build on the plot of wasteland, and we wondered who'd want to live next to the dual carriageway.

It got so hot by noon that we took a long break. We'd started work early in the morning when the sun was still low and red beyond the dewy fields. We walked over to the petrol station; there was a tap round the back which we used to freshen up.

Three men were sitting on the ground against the wall, their legs drawn up, their backs leaning on the concrete. They had water bottles in front of them, probably just filled up from the tap. They looked like Apaches sitting there like that, longish dark hair, but which of us had ever seen an Apache, except in films?

We went to get one of our Turkish guys – they were drinking coffee in the petrol station and they weren't actually Turkish at all – and he made himself understood somehow with the three men, who kept pointing at the patch of woods behind the petrol station. The middle one of the three was almost a child, still; he didn't look at us and he clutched his water bottle to his chest.

Our Turkish guy pointed at the woods too now, and we marched off to take a closer look.

A handful of women and men were sitting in a clearing. One of the women had scratched her face underneath her headscarf, and another woman was holding her arms down. They were squatting around a small boy lying on the forest floor. He had vomited blood and there were pine needles and grass and a bit of earth stuck around his mouth. We leaned over him but he was dead.

Our foreman used to work in forestry. He picked up a couple of wild flowers lying crushed next to the boy.

'Autumn crocuses,' he said, cautiously moving their pale pink petals. The boy must have eaten some of them.

We stood for a while around the boy and his family, come from far away to this patch of woods, and then we thought about whether to call the police or an ambulance or both. One of the women said something to us but we didn't understand her. Later, when the boy was in a van and we'd signed some papers or other, we went back to the petrol station and the stretch of land right next to the dual carriageway.

The day was long and hot, and we worked in silence until evening came.

BROKEN GLASS IN UNIT 95

The nights were dull and endless, started at six and ended at six, they were like dark days that touched in the middle, and when they stopped being dull they got even darker and more endless and we wished we were bored again, hours half-asleep between our inspection rounds, our heads never allowed to touch the table top, we'd doze sitting up, but Unit 95 had become unpredictable and some of us had got unpredictable too and lost our nerve and got taken off the job, but I tried to stay calm, I knew the new part of town, the satellite town where Unit 95 was, I knew the nights when people went crazy, I'd been working in Unit 95, been doing my rounds all over town since the mid-nineties, I knew the hostels the other guys sometimes called 'roach motels', where the asylum-seekers lived, no one had ever liked working shifts there, and now it was all getting even worse.

Some of the old guys at work said: It's all starting over again. And they were right, I remembered the time and the nights when it was dangerous and there was no counting on the police, 'the pigs' as we called them back then. It seemed a long time ago, seemed a long way away, and then I realized I was an *old guy* as well.

Unit 95 was in the middle of the 1970s blocks and the new high-rises of the satellite town.

The blocks from the seventies had all been done up, their once-grey concrete walls decorated with brightly coloured shapes and patterns, and by day I saw a lot of the pensioners who lived there looking out of the windows when the weather was good, their arms resting on cushions, though there wasn't much to see in the satellite town or in Unit 95.

But there was the refugees' reception centre. Some of

the guys at work said Unit 95 *was* the reception centre, the 'RC', but that wasn't right.

Unit 95 was a square of ten-storey concrete blocks, a large courtyard between the blocks, and the RC a bit further outside the square; a property company had bought it all and done it up years ago, and now someone had to look after it, the nights were long in the satellite town, and as usual they wanted to save money and had signed up one of the cheapest security firms even though the reception centre was part of the package they'd bought from the council. I don't want to put us down, we were a good team, cheap but good, and at least some of the guys knew what they were letting themselves in for when they put on the uniform.

I started my round without the dog, like I always did. It was still almost light and the dog had hip problems like most of the work dogs, he was an old Belgian Shepherd, well trained but with a slight limp, the onset of HD, hip dysplasia, and I didn't take him on my round until after midnight. He stayed in the security cabin until then and rested. Our cabin was right next to the road on a grass verge and the light was on from six till six – you couldn't turn it off – so everyone could see us. A security guy and a dog in a glowing Plexiglas cabin, and outside, the night.

'One to Twelve, One to Twelve, come in, over.'

I unclipped the radio from my belt. It was heavy and much too large and a better weapon than the rubber baton I also wore on my belt. The radio was a relic from another era, we had mobiles and smartphones and all that crap, but the radio sent out beeps and white noise in the frequencies of the night, it spoke to us through time and space as I saw *her* again that night in Unit 95.

But it wasn't her. How could it be her, unchanged and

so young, after more than twenty years?

'Twelve, go ahead.'

I started my first round without the dog. It was autumn. I touched the first magnetic tag against my guard patrol reader. A low beep. I put the black device back into the side pocket of my uniform jacket; it looked like an electric shocker. The walkie-talkie crackled and began to speak, and I heard the voice of the old dispatcher back at base, far away from the satellite town, on the western edge of the town proper, out of which the satellite town grew like... days that... I shook my head, too many rounds, too many shifts over the past few weeks.

'One calling Twelve,' came the dispatcher. We'd been waiting years for him to retire. They said he used to be a big gun in the secret service but ever since I'd known him, since I started working for the security firm, he'd looked like an old man.

'Twelve, go ahead.'

'All quiet in Unit 95, over?'

'Expecting something?' I asked into the radio and walked to the next checkpoint, fixed to a wall a few buildings along, next to a children's playground. There were two children playing there even though it was almost dark. They looked like they'd come over from the RC, straight black hair, dark skin, they usually came to play in the evening once the other children had gone. My patrol reader beeped quietly as I touched it to the magnetic tag. The two children sat down on the sand under the climbing frame and held hands. And they sat there, hand in hand.

'Nothing in the weather report, over,' said the old dispatcher. Then I heard the click of his lighter. A lot of the guys at work smoked like chimneys. I'd given it up ten years ago, or maybe seven or eight, and when I began my week's shift, which usually went on for five or six or seven days even though that meant I was overstepping the statutory weekly working hours, I'd empty the ashtray in our security cabin onto the gravelly ground outside. Only occasionally did I go over with the hundreds of fag-ends to one of the stone rubbish bins the property company had put up all over Unit 95, immovable.

'Then I'll trust the weather report, over,' I said. I heard the old dispatcher breathing or blowing out smoke, his nicotine-yellow finger on the transmission button, 'Have a good shift then, over and out.'

I had touched in at a few checkpoints before I slowly approached the RC. In the nights, and sometimes in the early evenings, but usually in the nights, people would gather outside the RC, mostly young lads. Some came from the buildings in Unit 95, others from the depths of the satellite town. Everything seemed quiet today though. Even though it was a Friday. Some of the pensioners had said hello to me in the courtyards between the blocks, a last few bits of shopping in a plastic bag, a chat outside the building, an evening cigarette by one of the stone bins. And behind the concrete blocks of Unit 95, before the red-black, dark-blue sky, rose the residential complexes of the satellite town. Slab constructions and grid squares from the days of socialism, all over for more than twenty-five years now. When I looked at the map fixed to one of the glass walls of our security cabin, I saw the parts of our town, I saw Unit 95 on the edge of the satellite town, right where the concrete sets in; I don't know who had stuck the map to the glass. Our units were marked with felt-tip pen and I'd done shifts in most of them by now, the industrial estates, the Mockau Centre at the other end of town with all the shops on two floors and the long corridors, where I stood outside the jeweller's window and looked at the stones and the rings in the light of the night-time display. Only the old Russian barracks where we'd guarded the vacant buildings for a long time had gone, torn down over the years.

I held onto the fence and looked at the open window on the ground floor where the young woman was sitting on the windowsill, watched her through the fence. She was sitting on the windowsill, her legs bent, her head resting on her knees. She looked out into the evening with the room's light behind her. I could make out some kind of poster on the wall, shelves, a sofa with a blue bag on it. I clutched the guard patrol reader so tightly I thought for a moment the plastic casing would splinter. Where was the patrol tag where I had to touch in?

She had red-brown, medium-length hair and her skin was very pale. She was frowning, I could see that much. Perhaps she was thinking about important things while she looked out into the night, in which I stood behind the fence and understood nothing. I laid my hand on the cool metal strips and looked at her face and her small nose, a button nose, such a nice word, but she didn't seem to see me. I don't know how long I stood there; at some point I heard voices behind me, voices getting louder, calls from the night, and I knew the weather report had got it wrong again, and then I saw something happening on the grass between the RC and the fence, more and more refugees coming out of the building, I moved my head, saw a mob of young lads and boys and old men between Unit 95 and the RC. And while I moved my eyes between the two groups in front of me, my hand still on the fence, something changed – was it the light? Did the moon rise and cast shadows, or did clouds draw in across the sky? I looked through the mesh of the fence again. Where was she? Where was the bright window she was sitting in?

She stood out amongst the dark-skinned and dark-haired residents standing behind the fence outside the reception centre. There were a few fair-skinned and fair-haired ones – it was the time of the Russian Germans who came to us from the gigantic collapsing empire, but most of them didn't end up in the hostels. Our beat ended at the fence. We were only responsible for the old barracks, abandoned by the Russians and the size of a small town. Grass grew in the narrow roads between the buildings and there was broken glass everywhere. Sometimes the roads got wider, and sometimes I thought I heard the clank of tank tracks on the cobblestones.

Our room was in a small tower right next to the main gate. There was a plug point for a fan heater, a rotting sofa we used for our fitful naps, sitting up, head against the back because our team's patrol car sometimes came by, there was a coffee machine on a table and piles of newspapers and magazines everywhere, hundreds of newspapers and magazines – what did we know about the net in those days?

A few of the window panes were still intact; we'd boarded the others up with cardboard. That was where we sat in the days and in the nights. Went on our rounds with the dogs, taking us up to the fence separating the Russian barracks from the reception centre. The buildings were crumbling away, even though the Russians, the Soviets, had only withdrawn two years ago.

I stood by the fence, my hand on the cool metal. Where was she? Where was the bright window in Unit 95? The dog must have sensed I was by his side but somewhere else entirely. He howled quietly and took a few tense steps and rubbed his collar against the fence, like he wanted to get rid of it.

I always picked up the dog at base, where he waited in a kennel, and took him to the barracks that the Russians had left two years before. I stroked the Belgian Shepherd's soft grey fur, and suddenly it was a young Belgian Shepherd again. No, even back then most of our dogs were old and unwanted, and only I was young, and her. But there wasn't a dog beside me, the dog was in the security cabin, Unit 95, and my hand moved through air, stroked the air.

We walked our daily round. We walked a few years with our dogs until they started to go lame, and then they took them away and our firm gave us new dogs we had to get used to, cheap, unwanted dogs from vanished and vanishing borders, we got the dogs' names muddled up and the dogs often walked confused and tense beside us, rubbed their collars against fences and walls like they wanted to get rid of them, I stood with the dog by the gate of the Russian barracks and started my round through that small town. Broken glass crunched beneath our feet.

It was spring. Was it spring? Later, I gave her a flower with a purple blossom. I gave her a flower later, it grew in the rubble between the buildings. A spring flower. It was often cold in the nights and our breath turned to steam in the empty rooms.

I walked with the dog along the roads of the old Russian barracks, went from patrol tag to patrol tag. I sometimes wondered who'd smashed all the windows when the Russians pulled out. Some nights I'd heard the smashing, hadn't left our room, I'd looked at the lit-up gate, all quiet over there, I'd heard the glass smashing some nights, it was usually all over again soon enough, and in the morning, on my first patrol before the next shift came, I inspected the damage, walked carefully with the dog over the shards all over the roads.

She was stood by the fence, her head leaned against the metal – that was how I saw her the first time. She was wearing a coat that was far too big for her.

I stood a few yards away. After the council opened the RC next to the empty barracks, we had to touch in to a patrol tag along there too, on one of the fence pillars. 'The Russians left, the Yugos came,' the guys at work said.

She had red-brown, medium-length hair and her face was very pale, the skin on her hands was almost white too, and for a moment I thought maybe she worked in the RC; she didn't look like one of the dark asylum-seekers in the 'roach motel'. I used the word now and then too, when we were having coffee, before my shift finished and the next guy's shift began, just the way you talk sometimes so you don't look weak, even though I never had a problem with the asylum-seekers.

She had red-brown, medium-length hair, her forehead resting on the fence, and when she raised her head and looked at me, I saw the mesh of the fence had pressed its pattern into her skin there.

Even her eyes were pale, blue as I saw later, but sometimes it seemed, later when she vanished into memories, like her eyes got darker then, opened dark and enlarged, like the colour of water changes when the sky clouds over or the evening comes.

It wasn't just the too-big coat she was wearing, the rolled-up sleeves slipping over her hands again and again that made her look strangely lost and small, even though she wasn't all that small as she leaned against the fence like that, as I went up closer to her and looked at her. How old might she be, eighteen? Nineteen? The dog ran ahead, tugged at the lead, wanted to go to her, even though I kept saying 'Heel'. Maybe he remembered the fences at the borders where he'd worked. I wanted to put the leather muzzle that I always carried with me on him but he was already at the fence, and the girl squatted down and pushed her hand through the mesh, and the dog sniffed at her hand and flapped his big tongue onto her fingers until I pulled him away. 'Stop it!'

She looked up at me. 'No,' she said. 'Dog good.' And again, the dog tugged at the lead and went to her, and she smiled because it looked like he was wrapping his big tongue around her hand.

'Hello,' I said.

'Hello, Mr Officer,' she said. She spoke with an accent, like the Russians, the Soviet soldiers, spoke before they were withdrawn.

'I'm not an officer,' I said.

She stood back up and I went up close to the fence, and she patted her shoulders with both hands and said, 'You officer.'

I felt one of the epaulettes on my blue uniform jacket. I smiled and said, 'I'm just security.'

'Ah, Securitate, you make sure we not bad.' She pushed her hand through the fence again and tapped me on the chest.

'No,' I said and looked past her at the low-rise, metal-cladded buildings of the RC, a few people sitting outside, some of them on plastic chairs, men standing around a large mushroom-shaped ashtray and smoking, windows were open, an old lady was leaning on a cushion on her windowsill, brightly coloured clothes hung up to dry in some of the open windows. 'My army's only there.' I turned around and pointed at the abandoned barracks behind me.

'You officer!' she said. Then she turned and went

back to one of the buildings. As I was about to leave too, she stopped again. 'Your dog,' she called out, 'your dog very...' she hesitated. '*Krasivaya*,' she said, but not as loud, I could barely understand her this time, '*krasivaya*'.

'Beautiful,' I said, and then again, slightly louder: 'Beautiful,' and I saw her smile, then she turned away and walked on, the coat dragging along the ground behind her like a train. My Russian wasn't that great, I'd never been good at it at school and school was a few years back now, but '*krasivaya*', that much I understood. I touched in to the patrol tag I'd almost forgotten and walked back to the roads of the barracks, back to the broken glass.

When I met her a few days later by the fence, she asked me the dog's name.

'Your dog no name, no?'

'We call him number three,' I said. 'And you, what's your name?'

'Number three? Dog needs name.'

'You can call him whatever you like. If you tell me your...'

The dog had settled down quietly on the ground next to me, tired.

She didn't answer, didn't tell me her name. She looked at the dog and then me, she leaned against the fence, her arms spread wide and her fingers locked around the wire, and she lifted her feet, bent her legs backwards a bit, like a girl hanging off a climbing frame. 'I had dog too,' she said, 'at home.'

'And... where is that, where was that?' I took a step closer, our faces now directly in front of each other, only the metal mesh of the fence between us.

'We had dog too,' she said again and looked past me through the grid of the fence at the slowly crumbling

24

buildings of the old barracks.

'You're from Russia,' I said. 'From the big Soviet Union.'

'Not Russia,' she said, 'small country, very far. And mountains. Our village... near the mountains.' She moved both hands like she was shaping giant mountains, and then she put her palms side by side, facing downwards, as though the village she came from was there, on her hands, at the foot of the mountains, in the valley. We sat on the steps leading to the roofed entrance to the old officers' mess. I had let the dog off the leash and he sniffed at a couple of walls, then lay down in a patch of sunlight on the cobbles of the little road.

'It's funny,' I said, 'he's actually a... a sharp dog...'

'What is... sharp dog?' She didn't understand.

'I mean, he... had to be fierce, back then, on the border, with the police, *granitsa, politsiya... panimayesh*?'

'He old now, want peace.'

'Maybe,' I said. *'Moshet.'*

'Your Russian good,' she said.

'I learned it at school, you know, in the old days. But I speak much too little, much too small. *Malyi, malyi.'*

'My dog name was Gigi.'

'That's a nice name for a dog.'

'Yes?' She smiled. 'I call him that, but Papa say...' She stopped talking, and we were quiet for a while and watched the dog dozing in the sun.

'Your German very good,' I said.

'Too little,' she said, *'malyi, malyi.'*

'No, Marika,' I said, 'you speak good German, you... very beautiful.' She looked at me, a crease above her small nose all the way up to her forehead. I couldn't help smiling, and then I laughed – sometimes you say these things, you're so stupid and clumsy it's like you suddenly turn back into a boy, a schoolboy, a child.

'You laugh at me.'

'No, Marika, I never laugh at you. You are...'

'Little officer always love women, no?' She slid one finger under one of the epaulettes on my uniform jacket and tugged slightly at the blue fabric.

She had stopped in her tracks after we'd met at the fence the second time and she'd turned back to the RC buildings.

I had touched in to the patrol tag and she had turned around, and she looked very helpless and very lost as she stood there halfway between the fence and the housing facility. I could see her hands stroking over the fabric of her coat, up and down. She was standing very straight and pressing her arms to her sides, and then she came back a few steps towards the fence and told me her name.

She was still wearing the too-big coat, its sleeves rolled up but still always slipping down over her hands. 'You scared in the night, no?'

'Yes,' I said, 'no, I mean, he looks out for me,' I pointed at the dog, still dozing in the last rays of evening sunshine, 'and I... I'm a specialist, and what would happen here anyway?'

'Yes,' she said after a while, 'nothing,' but I could tell she was somewhere else entirely. She'd let go of my epaulette and leaned forwards and rested her elbows on her knees, her arms crossed in front of her chest, her hands gripping her upper arms. She looked at the house opposite, a brick building, the bricks dark red and black in places, and the windows were smashed like almost all windows in the old barracks, and the broken glass was scattered on the road and the narrow footpath.

Cautiously, I touched the fabric of her coat, put my hand on her bent back, below the back of her neck, so she knew I was there. She's somewhere else. She looked at the broken windows.

I saw her lips whispering something, was it names? But I didn't understand. 'Marika,' I said and leaned forward, squatted down in front of her and tried to look her in the eye, her head bent low. Her blue eyes seemed to get darker now, her pupils huge, and I got up, had to look away because I was scared of getting lost in them. I don't know how long she sat there just gently rocking her upper body, whispering to herself. I'd lit my cigarette, the dog trotted over to the gate, to our staffroom that we weren't supposed to leave in the nights, probably the firm didn't want any trouble if we broke our necks in the dark, half-derelict buildings... and then she was standing next to me.

'Dog dead,' she whispered as she leaned against me.

I put my arm around her and said, 'Everything... everything's fine.'

'No,' she said, 'nothing fine.'

'Yes,' I said, 'maybe. But now, you... you're...'

'Yes,' she said, 'now I'm here. You good.'

'*Mala* Marika.' I pressed her to me and we stood like that for a while and watched the sky turn red behind the old barracks buildings and grey clouds drift through the red, then the sky grew dark, it had turned cool, and she clutched her too-big coat together over her chest, and then I walked her to the end of the fence, where it looked like the fence joined up with a brick wall but there was a gap there, between wall and fence.

I sat in our staffroom all night and smoked. I only had a few cigarettes in a leather case because I didn't smoke much on the job, one or two cigarettes, and when the next guy came in the morning for his shift he and I would smoke one or two cigarettes together, talk about this and that or not say anything, before I went home.

A few times I fell asleep, woke up again and blinked at the semi-dark room, but she didn't come. I went down to the gate and did my midnight patrol touch-in and gave the iron chain a quick shake before I went back up. The hum of a distant motorway, the lights of the town, the strange smell of spring. I wrote in the duty book: *Nothing to report*. Flicked through the duty book, read the other guys' notes. *Children on the property, vandals at 1 am, informed HQ, scrap metal scavengers on the property, informed HQ...*

The dog lay on his mat, asleep. I took my Maglite and went down to the ground floor. There was a little room there. Glass crunched beneath my shoes, only a little light falling from the staircase into the empty room, I squatted down and undid my trousers. She'd kissed me before she'd crawled through the gap between wall and fence.

I was ashamed when I went back upstairs. But I'd been so wound up. Her hand on my face. 'You come back... tomorrow?' Her turning around and smiling. And raising her hand. And waving. 'How old are you, Marika?'

'Nineteen.'

'And your parents?'

She doesn't reply, resting her head on her hands. She has medium-length red-brown hair and a mole on the back of her neck – I can feel it when I run my hands through her hair.

Her turning away when I want to kiss her, and then her kissing me before she vanishes onto the RC grounds, behind the fence.

I walked up the stairs. Then I turned around again and went to the door, opened it and leaned against the doorframe. Ahead of me, the barracks, all the buildings in deep darkness. Only the big iron gate was lit up. The RC wasn't visible from there; they were all bound to be asleep there now. Was *she* asleep? Or lying awake and staring at the ceiling, or standing by the window?

Just a brief kiss, no hesitation. The fabric of her too-big coat. The gap between fence and wall. I walked to the fence every day but she wasn't there. The nights were dull and endless. The broken glass in the beam of my Maglite, drops shone like milk on the broken glass, I stood in the doorway and smoked my last cigarette, still wound up, I kept going to the fence, always in the hour before dusk, I picked up one of the shards and held it up.

'One calling Twelve, One to Twelve, come in, over!'

I don't know how long I'd been standing by the fence. I'd pressed my head against the metal mesh, and when I wiped my damp forehead I felt the pattern, the imprint on my skin. I turned around. Behind me, police forcing the crowd back. Flashing blue lights, a few police cars. How long had I been here at the fence? Then I saw a few young lads appearing out of the darkness from one side, the tall blocks of the satellite town behind them. What were they doing there? It looked like they were doing gymnastics, contortions, night-time gymnasts, but then I heard the crash as one of the cobblestones slammed against the façade of the RC, and I turned around to them slowly – where was my dog? – and another stone went flying, me following the curve of its trajectory in confusion, and again one of the men contorted his body. There was a smash. A couple of policemen ran over to the stone-throwers. The light switched off in the RC. I walked slowly to the gate. The window I'd seen her in was dark now. I heard the crowd's shouts behind me. The voices rang out through the night as though they were hitting the façade and bouncing off it before they reached me, I could feel it, as though the air pressure around me was changing, over and over, word by word, sentence by sentence.

'You have to look after me, little officer, no?'

'You... you don't need to be scared any more, Marika.'

'I waited, I...'

'I'm here again now.'

'That's good.'

I didn't ask her where she'd been when I'd waited by the fence, day after day. She was back again now. And our voices rang out in the big empty officers' mess, almost like echoes. 'Marika... officer... no... not alone.'

I'd had shifts in other properties, the Mockau Centre had just opened and we patrolled there, checked on the shops and restaurants, stood outside the metal shutters of the jeweller's guessing at the glint of the jewellery and diamonds behind them, or was it just cheap crap and cut-price stuff? The Mockau Centre was on the edge of town, where the houses were crumbling and a few isolated concrete blocks, fifteen floors high, grew strangely scattered up to the sky. Between our rounds, when we drank coffee in our staffroom in the basement, we sometimes listened in to the radio communication between headquarters and the other guys to pass the time, 'Better than the top ten!' my workmate said, and that was how I found out there were incidents at the RC again. 'Copy that, Nine... It's not part of the unit, informing the police...'

I had gone out to our firm car and driven through the empty streets of the city to the RC. My workmate was still in our staffroom at the Mockau Centre, his head on the tabletop, asleep. He liked a splash of something extra in his coffee and he wouldn't say anything if I popped out for a bit.

I sat in the car, a little way away from the RC, saw the blue flashes of the police vehicles, a couple of bone-heads walking along the pavement on the other side of the road. The show must be over and the pigs had been pretty lax, as usual, you still saw real boneheads back then, you could spot them a mile off, I saw a big coach alongside the RC, people getting on it, for a moment I thought I saw *her*, in her coat that was far too big for her.

She was clutching the lapels of her coat together like she was cold. Small dark stains on the fabric, up on the collar. It was an old dark-grey men's coat but the stains were even darker than the fabric.

'Soviet long ago, no?'

'Yes, very long,' I said.

'When the Soviets go from us, war began.'

We were leaning against a long wooden counter, behind it the remains of shelves. The glass in the tall windows was all smashed, and the evening light fell through rags of curtain onto the scratched wooden floor. The room was completely empty except for a table, knocked over onto its side. We leaned our backs against the bar and looked at the opposite wall, at the relics of a large mosaic, a picture made of thousands of little tiles. We could still make out half a red star, parts of soldiers with Kalashnikovs, but most of it had been broken off – night-time vandals, children, drunk scavengers. I don't know how long we stood there and stared at the wrecked picture in silence.

'Sometimes I hear a soldier at night,' I said. 'Russki, Soviet.'

'Here? A joke, no?'

'He sings here, Marika, he stayed behind. He sings soldiers' songs. And when I check in the morning there are butts on the counter, cigarettes...'

31

She laughed and tugged at the epaulette on my uniform jacket. 'You make joke, little German officer.' She touched my face with her fingertips. '*You* smoke cigarettes here, in evening, *vecherom*...'

'*Vecherom*,' I said, and put my hand on hers. She'd turned up out of the blue outside the staffroom, standing in the middle of the little road, and I saw her from the window. She seemed scared, and even though she pressed up against me there was something strange and cool about her, she was elsewhere, so I didn't dare to kiss her, to touch her...

'Papirossi,' I said, 'look, here,' I pointed at the extinguished cigarettes with the long Russian papirossi filters on the floor around us, 'they're original Russian papirossis. A soldier stayed here, he lives in the cellar, and sometimes I hear him singing.'

'Papirossi,' she said and stroked my face, and my hand, still on hers, moved with her hand. 'My father smoke papirossi, at home. Once, I still child, I tried. But too strong, I feel sick, so sick... and Papa shouted...'

She pulled her hand away, no, she hadn't stroked my face, she wanted to remove her hand from under mine. A brief kiss by the fence, uncertain, and my lips brushed against her nose. She clutched her coat together over her chest, like she was cold. I didn't have to look her in the eye, I knew she was somewhere else again. At home. *Doma*, as she said in Russian, even though she wasn't Russian. The big, collapsed Soviet Union. She had never answered when I asked about her parents. There was nothing I could do, except wait. I looked for my cigarette case in the pockets of my uniform jacket.

'Papirossi old,' she said suddenly, bending down and picking up one of the cigarette ends, cautiously reaching two fingers out for the slim, long-yellowed filter. She picked the cigarette up, held it up in the air for a moment, between us, then flicked it away.

'You telling... *skazka*...'

'Stories,' I said.

'Yes,' she said. 'No soldier here.'

'No,' I shook my head. 'No soldier.'

'But you here, officer,' she said, and her voice trembled slightly, and she smiled and turned around to me, 'we drink *krimskoye*,' she raised her hand as if to order from the man behind the bar, 'today my birthday.'

She stepped in front of me and took me by the shoulders and pulled me into the middle of the room, where the dance floor must once have been.

'Come,' she said, 'we dance.'

We danced in silence, uncertain to begin with, feeling for a rhythm, feeling for music, only the sound of our feet on the floor. We danced very slowly, I pulled her very close, felt her breasts rising and falling when she breathed and as we turned, still dancing, towards the tall windows, the evening light falling through them, the shards crunching beneath our feet. She rested her head on my shoulder. I was only a tiny bit taller than her and when I tilted my head slightly my face touched her red-brown hair. We lost the beat because we had to dance around the upturned table, we danced slower and slower, our hands on each other's backs, and pressed up against each other, and sometimes we felt the light falling through the windows, and then it was gone again; we moved around the room, her humming some tune or other, her lips on my shirt, we moved in the light, we danced until it grew dark and the sun had set between the roofs of the old Russian barracks.

The room was in darkness. She went to the window and I could make out her red-brown hair in the sparse light. Nothing had changed. Somewhere there was a war again, which had brought her back to me.

'What happened to your parents?'

'*Ya ne znayu.*'

'Your mother?'

'*Ya ne znayu.*'

'Mama, *tebya mama*?' I hadn't spoken Russian since the old days and I had to search for the words and search for the sentences.

'I not...' She stood by the window with her back to me, she didn't want me to turn on the light. She was scared, even though it was quiet outside now, only one police car parked outside the RC. A policeman leaning against the car, another had wound the window down, only his arm visible hanging over the edge, a cigarette between his fingers.

'I... I not...'

'No, you not. Marika.'

'Marika?' She turned back to me. She'd be maybe nineteen or twenty. She had her arms crossed over her chest and she was trembling a little.

I asked her where she came from, told her the small country with the mountains, the valleys, the one she'd once talked about. But she didn't answer. She looked at me with her big eyes, their blue seeming to get darker, like the colour of water changes, darkens, when the sky clouds over or when the evening comes.

But perhaps it was just the dusky light in the room.

'Your mother,' I said, '*vasha mama...*'

'No,' she said, '*nyet. Ya ne znayu...*'

'No,' I said, 'no, no. *Vasha mama, eto Marika? Gdye Marika?*' I had tried to find out where she was, back then when she vanished, but there was no point and I soon gave up.

'I not Marika,' she said. *'Ya ne panimayu...'* and she took a few more steps back to the window.

The poster on the wall was a large calendar with Arabic characters over some kind of kitsch desert landscape with a mosque. She must have been sharing the room, or it was already there when she arrived.

I walked the path back to the fence. The police car was still parked outside the RC, the two police officers sitting inside it, the windows closed, and it looked like they were asleep in their seats.

Broken glass crunched beneath my feet, a window had shattered, up on the second floor, the room behind it dark and empty. I bent down and picked up one of the shards.

'You always Securitate officer?'

'No.'

'You still young...'

'You're still young, Marika.'

'We both young, little officer.'

'Yes, we both.'

I threw the shard into the darkness and went back into Unit 95, to the silent high-rises of the satellite town, where the dog was waiting in our cabin, or asleep. I stopped again at the fence. For a moment, I thought I saw her, the small nose, button nose, a nice word, her medium-length red-brown hair...

I sat in the car and stared at the coach as the men, women and children got on.

Were they being transferred? Evacuated? The blue glow of the police cars. I sat in our firm car until the morning came.

'One calling Twelve, over.'

'Twelve, go ahead.'

'You're getting sloppy, Ms Fischer.'

'Yes,' she said. 'No...'

'So you admit you're getting sloppy, Ms Fischer.'

'No,' she said. 'I just had a bad day, I—'

'You've been working here long enough, you know we can't afford complaints.'

'Yes,' she said, 'it won't happen—'

'It most certainly won't. We're counting on you, you're part of our team. But if you can't keep up, we do understand.'

'No,' she said, 'I can keep up, it was just—'

'Not to worry, Ms Fischer, anyone can have a bad day.'

She held the two cherry stones in her clenched fist for the whole walk alongside the tracks to the station. She was wearing her luminous orange hi-vis vest over her blue dungarees, like she always did when she walked along the tracks to the station after the afternoon shift. In the onsetting night, she saw the arches leading into the huge station building like gateways. The tracks shimmered reddish and in some places silver in the dusk, it was early September, and the remains of the day still dimmed late when the sky was clear.

She threw her cloth bag with the eleven empty deposit bottles into a bush beside the tracks. Then she turned back and tried to tug the bag out of the brushy, thorny bush. She squatted down by the bush and she heard a train, the clank and hum of the branching and crossing tracks, but she knew the train was far enough away.

She put her fist down on the bar. Opened it and felt the two cherry stones falling out. No, she'd been clenching her fist so tightly as she walked alongside the tracks to the station that one stone stuck for a moment to the skin of her palm. She'd abandoned the bag in the tangled bush after all. Even though the bottles were worth two seventy-five. But the supermarket in the station basement was closing in a few minutes and she didn't want to run. It had been a long hard day with a long evening on the trains. She could have taken the bag of bottles home with her but she didn't feel like sitting on the tram with a beer-soaked bag after that middle shift. And she had thrown the bag away in anger because she could still hear the Chief Cleaning Inspector's voice. It chattered away beside her over the railway sleepers, 'You're – getting – sloppy...' screeched the brakes of the trains as they entered the station, left the station. She went back for the bag the next day.

'And do you know what else we found?'

'Apart from the two cherry stones? Bet it wasn't your wrinkly old balls.'

She laughed and drank a sip of her coffee. She'd tipped a *small Maria* into the cup, a small glass of Mariacron brandy. The station pub was right next to the staircase leading down from the platforms to the lower West concourse. When she turned around she could see through the long, narrow pub windows to the hairdresser's on the other side of the big staircase. A room made of glass, hood dryers standing in a semi-circle. Two young women finishing off for the night in the bright light, clearing up, sweeping the cut hair off the floor, time to go now, after ten already. Later, the dryers stood in the dark as the station prepared for the night, the last trains, shadows on the platforms, last travellers climbing the stairs to the platforms. She heard the screech of trams in the forecourt as security guards passed the pub, always in pairs, night shift, time to go home. The dryers stood in the dark and she turned back to the bar.

'Another small Maria?' The chubby pub landlord was already holding the bottle of Mariacron brandy and smiling at her over his round metal-rimmed glasses, looking more like a friendly primary school teacher than a publican. She nodded and laid her hand over the cherry stones. For a few years now, she'd been going for a drink in the station pub now and then after the middle shift, but she didn't know the landlord's name. Klaus? No. Jimmy the Wasp? No, that was a whole 'nother story.

Sometimes his wife ran the place, a heavy smoker with her hair already half grey, and sometimes, when the place was busy, at weekends or over Christmas, they were both behind the bar.

She sipped at her small Maria. She couldn't take much alcohol; it made her tired. She sipped at her small Maria, closed her eyes and listened to the strange sounds of the station by night. Someone shouted something some-where – it echoed beneath the dome, between the arches. The pub had two doors, usually open except in winter when the cold came in with the trains through the great gateways. The station would steam, then, sending steam out into the darkness while she strode towards it along-side the tracks after the middle shift, as though it were breathing out through the great arches, as though its breath were freezing in the cold. She'd trudge along-side the track, trudge through the snow, deposit bottles clinking in the bag hitting her leg. Another ten min-utes before the supermarket on the ground floor closed. Fifteen bottles, three seventy-five.

Good thing there aren't that many winter days and winter nights any more, she thought as she approached the station's arches. The yellow light of the platforms mixing with the white breath. She could barely see her own breath. She clenched her fists, her work gloves still on. She opened and closed her palms over and over to ward off the cold, made a fist that she opened and then closed again.

'Excuse me, you've dropped something.'

'What?' She opened her eyes and turned around. There was a woman at one of the tables behind her.

The woman pointed at the floor. 'You just dropped something.' The woman had dark hair, shiny and black like patent leather, presumably dyed because she had to be in her early sixties. Her face was gaunt and when she took a drag on her cigarette it looked like the wrinkles around the edges of her mouth got deeper and longer.

'Oh, thanks.' She looked at the floor but she couldn't see anything there. She got up from her bar stool to bend over.

'Hold on, right there next to the chair leg.' The other woman stood up too and they almost bumped heads.

'Sorry,' said the dark-haired woman, and took a step back. 'There, it's down there, you just dropped it...'

And now she saw the cherry stone. The other one was still on the bar next to her small Maria. She squatted down and picked up the cherry stone between finger and thumb. Standing up, she felt the pain in her back again, right above her tailbone, that had been troubling her for days. 'Thank you, but it's... it's nothing much.' She put the cherry stone in the ashtray a little way from her small Maria on the bar.

'Is it a...' said the dark-haired woman, walking slowly over to her at the bar. 'It looked like a pearl.' She held her cigarette slightly behind her, one arm away from her body as though she didn't want to bother her with the smoke.

'A pearl?' she said, and felt herself smiling. 'No, afraid not.'

The dark-haired woman extinguished her cigarette in the ashtray where the cherry stone now was.

'The smoke doesn't bother me,' she said to the dark-haired woman. 'It's a smoking bar. And I like the smell.'

'You're from the smoking days too,' said the dark-haired woman, and nodded.

'The smoking days,' she said. 'Yes...' and she nodded too and looked out through the window past the dark-haired woman at the semi-dark station concourse empty below them, and then she saw the mini bottle of sparkling wine on the table by the window.

'Your drink,' she said and turned back to the bar, 'you've forgotten your drink.'

'Thanks,' said the dark-haired woman. 'Don't mind if I do.' She got up, fetched the bottle and the tall, thin glass and put them down next to the ashtray. 'Cheers,' she said, raising her half-full sparkling wine, and then they clinked glasses.

The small Maria was almost gone and she waved over the fat man whose name she'd forgotten and ordered another shot.

'You used to smoke?' asked the woman with the dark hair that shone like patent leather, topping up her glass from the miniature bottle.

'No, my husband smoked,' she said, 'and I miss it sometimes.'

And they both nodded again and fell silent and looked somewhere, past each other, at the glass panes that reflected the inside of the station pub back at them, the other tables and chairs, the chubby landlord topping someone up, the chubby landlord who looked like a teacher, round glasses slipping down a nose shining with sweat, beer foam on pint glasses, a man leaning into the slot machine on the other side of the room and putting more money in it and the bright lights of the slot machine flickering on his face, smoke above the square of the bar, a man eating a sausage at one table, the radio so low they could barely hear it.

'So you work for Deutsche Bahn?' asked the dark-haired woman, reaching into the inside pocket of her summer coat.

'Why d'you ask?' she asked, and then she remembered she was still wearing her orange safety vest, and then the dark-haired woman tapped at the lapels of her summer coat to remind her of the vest, and she got angry with herself and said very loudly, 'Yes, OK, I know.'

'Sorry,' said the dark-haired woman. 'I didn't mean to...'

'Never mind,' she said, and took a sip of her small Maria and sensed that she was already slightly drunk, and she shook her head, trying to shake the small Marias out of it before she went on – she didn't usually drink this much.

'I always take it off, usually,' she said. 'I always have a bag with me for putting this orange firecracker in.'

'It suits you,' said the dark-haired woman, and looked at her and then lowered her eyes and took a pack of cigarettes out of the inside pocket of her summer coat. 'Why do you want to take it off now?'

'Because I've finished work,' she said, and took off the vest and put it on the bar stool between them. 'Sorry about just now...'

'No, don't be,' said the woman with the dark hair and the summer coat, scuffed and threadbare at the sleeves and elbows. 'I understand. When I leave work, I want to... leave my work behind, too.'

'Where do *you* work?' she asked, and sipped at her small Maria and felt calmer again and her head clearer.

The woman with the dark hair and the threadbare but still elegant summer coat blew out smoke, and she breathed it in and smelled the cigarette smoke. She loved smoking along like that; her husband had smoked a lot – hadn't she even told the other woman that, earlier? All the things you tell people in the night. After the middle shift. They came from the smoking days.

'At the hairdresser's.'

'What?'

'You asked me where I work.'

'Yes. Oh, you work right over there?' She lowered her head to the big window with the staircase behind it, leading down into the West concourse. The hairdresser's on the other side of the stairs. The semi-circle of dryers.

'No, not over there,' the dark-haired woman smiled and tapped her cigarette with her forefinger, sending the ash down to the glass ashtray. 'Only young things work in there. Super Cut – no, they'd never take me.'

'Super Cut? What a stupid name.' She lowered her head and read the writing on the other side of the staircase. 'I've never been in there. I always go to the place round the corner from me.'

'Whereabouts do you live?'

'Schönefeld. Always have.'

'Schönefeld – beautiful field.'

She laughed at that. 'No, not these days. Hoffmann's Hairdressing. Do you know it? A really old salon.'

'Hoffmann's, yes.' The woman with the dark hair and the summer coat nodded and put out her cigarette. 'It really has been going a long time. I used to know old Mrs Hoffmann.'

'The one with the wonky nose?'

'No, that's her daughter. Is the place still going strong?'

'Well, young Mrs Hoffmann's not young any more and it's not easy. But as long as *I'm* still going there...' She laughed and ran her hands through her hair and remembered she hadn't been to Hoffmann's Hairdressing for a long time.

'I work over there in the East concourse,' said the woman with the dark hair and the summer coat, 'by the other staircase.'

'I often pass by,' she said, and sipped at her small Maria again even though the glass was empty now. 'It seems to be a good, quiet salon.'

'We don't have music blaring all day long like they do, anyway.' The dark-haired woman nodded towards the staircase, towards Super Cut. 'We're a clean, quiet, well-run business. That place over there is nothing but chaos – I can tell straight away just from walking past.'

And a little later, the two of them are outside the clean, quiet, well-run business by the staircase to the East concourse. The station is abandoned now. Night beneath the arches. Trains on some platforms. She knows her workmates from the night shift are going through the carriages. In the station and out on the sidings. The dark-haired woman reaches into the side pocket of her summer coat, which looks very elegant in the dim station light, almost French. She's a little envious of the woman: of her coat, her dark hair... She touches the coarse fabric of her shapeless blue dungarees.

A mobile had rung in the summer coat. 'Something's buzzing,' she'd said, and the dark-haired woman had answered the call.

'I have to go back over,' she said, then.

'Left something behind?' she asked.

'No, the light. Someone left the light on, and that someone must have been me.'

'Worse things happen at sea.'

'Yes. A friend of the boss saw it and called my boss,' she said.

'But you can't hardly see anything,' she said as she and the hairdresser stood outside the clean, quiet, well-run hairdressing salon by the staircase to the East concourse.

The only light to be seen was a weak yellow glow somewhere at the back of the shop. They were outside the large shop window. Hood dryers in a row along one wall. In the yellow light, casting strange shadows behind the big window, it looked for a moment as though there were customers sitting waiting under some of the hoods. She clutched her folded safety vest to her chest and the hairdresser said nothing either, and they stood like that for a while and stared at the big shop window, behind which the yellow light sparsely illuminated the salon, empty mirrors facing empty chairs... 'There's this lamp, just a standing lamp, and I always leave it on when I finish off. When I've switched everything off. When I lock everything up. My boss always says, don't forget the light. Costs electricity.'

'That's rubbish with the electricity. Pennies. Deposit money.'

'Deposit money?'

'Forget it. I just meant, I often leave the hall light on before I go to sleep. It's on all night. So what? What does that cost? Nothing. Sod it.'

'Is it calming?'

'Is what calming?'

'The light in the hall.'

'It's good to see it through the crack in the door.'

'I'll just pop in, if you want to wait...'

'I have to run, the last tram.'

'You were going to tell me about the cherry stones...'

'The cherry stones? I want to plant them, in the garden of the block where I live. Two cherry trees. And then I'll be a cherry-seller.'

'A cherry-seller? You say the craziest things...'

The dark-haired woman shook her head and unlocked the salon door, went inside.

She waved at her before she went down the stairs to the East concourse, and the dark-haired woman waved back from behind the door, and then she walked slowly, one step at a time, down to the concourse. 'Why didn't you want to tell me the thing about the cherry stones the other day?'

'Because it's not true. They found them under a seat, on the trains, the inspection commission.'

'Inspection commission? You're kidding?'

'No.'

'You should plant them, you really should.'

'You see, that was a much nicer idea. But you insisted.' And as she walked slowly across the East concourse to the exit, to the tram stop, she turned back around and saw the light going out behind the big window by the staircase.

She saw her behind the big window. The dark-haired woman crossed the hairdressing salon, a little unsure, as though she had just woken up.

She had taken off the orange safety vest and was clutching it to her chest. She saw the dark-haired woman putting on her white work coat. It was just after six in the morning, the end of the night shift on the trains, the start of the early shift in the salon. She'd swept and wiped all night, her workmates taciturn in the morning hours and everything difficult, and it seemed as though the trains they worked on got longer and longer, a new carriage waiting after every one they'd cleaned.

At first, she hadn't wanted to walk back to the station, alongside the tracks, after she and her workmates had stopped off at the maintenance building where the shifts began and ended, by the side of the tracks, but then she'd put her orange safety vest back on and marched off. The morning was dark and grey, as though still night. She was wearing a jumper under her blue dungarees now; after the night shift they stowed the deposit bottles and cans they found on the trains in the cleaning services building and divided them up later.

The first trains pulled into the station, drizzle in the air, a wet grey morning, and the tracks glinted silver in the light of the illuminated carriages, the trains clanked and rumbled over the tangle of rails and into the great gates beneath the arches of the dome. As she finally reached the outside platform, rising up ahead of her like a giant step, she felt her back twinge again. She squatted down and ran her broom beneath the seats, no cherry stones in among all the rubbish she swept out. 'You're getting sloppy, Ms Fischer.' She swept for half the night, then she took over the train windows. She dunked the wiper in the bucket, leaned forward and touched the glass with the wet window wiper, running it across the glass. She felt her back twinge and swayed along the outside platform. 'You know what, you walk like a sailor.'

'Me, like a sailor? I don't...'

'You do, like a sailor just going on land.'

'I'm not some old sea dog...'

'Like a first officer just going on land.'

'You're not making it any better!'

'But I like the way you walk. I like watching it.'

At six in the morning the station was full of people, filling up with commuters, workers, travellers, and she regretted not going straight from the cleaning services building to the tram stop. But then she saw the glass walls of the hairdressing salon, far off still, and she raised a hand as though to say hello, although she didn't even know if she was behind the glass and setting up for the day shift, and the salon was still so far away that her hand covered the whole window, and she put her hands back in the pockets of her blue work overalls and walked, slowly and swaying a little, past the morning people. She took the shortcut through a tunnel beneath the platforms, a subterranean link between the platforms. She liked the tunnel – there was usually no one else there. Only a few travellers and station people used the shortcut. She stopped for a moment and looked along the sparsely lit tube, in which her steps would echo again any minute now; she liked the sounds down there too. The footsteps bouncing off the walls, the echo when she coughed. She always wondered why the punks who sat drinking outside the entrances didn't use the tunnel, the homeless and the foreigners who stood around the station and often crisscrossed the concourses, why they didn't come down for a little peace or to do their dirty business. She never saw the station security men down there.

She walked along the tunnel underneath the platforms, heard the trains rumbling above the bricks and mortar, walked past the steel doors leading deep into the ground on either side, who knows where to, and then she slowly climbed the steps to platform eleven. And then she saw her behind the big shop window. She was putting on her white work tunic and setting everything up for the day shift in the salon. And she stood there on platform eleven and watched her and heard the train to Berlin pulling in, and all the early-morning travellers dashed past her, and she took off her orange safety vest and walked between them with the orange safety vest clutched to her chest, swaying a little after the long night.

She leaned against one of the yellow timetables and watched her bending over the row of hood dryers and switching the lights on, and she saw her reflected in the many mirrors.

They hadn't seen each other for a few weeks but their shifts would be ending together again soon. How often had they met now, three or four times?

'Christa Fischer.'

'Birgitt.'

'And your surname?'

'Why?'

'I told you mine...'

'Krentz.'

'Like the politician?'

'No, with t-z.'

'Thank God for that. That old Krenz was a real blue-shirted commie. Egon, the chief of the blue-shirts.'

'I was a blue-shirt too. I was really into the Free German Youth as a girl, back in the GDR.'

'Me too, Birgitt. But it's decades ago now. We were probably all young communists.'

'Socialists.'

'Yes, pretty young socialists, whatever. Blue-shirts. And I still have to wear that same shade of blue overalls to work.'

'Blue you,' said Birgitt, the woman with dark hair. They were sitting at the bar, sharing a miniature bottle of sparkling wine. They looked tired, their heads resting on their hands, their elbows on the wood of the bar.

'Oh yes,' said Christa Fischer, 'I'm a working-class heroine.'

And later, and nights and weeks had passed and before – how often had they met now? – shortly before the station pub by the staircase leading down to the West concourse closed, midnight, they heard the song 'Lady in Black' on the radio.

'I used to dance to this one at the disco.'

'Me too. A hundred years ago.'

'Do you understand the words?'

'Not really. She came one morning. And then something about winter wind.'

'It'll be winter soon enough.'

'Shall we share another bottle?'

'Yes, let's.' And Birgitt, the hairdresser, ordered another miniature bottle of sparkling wine and two glasses.

'That's the last round,' said the chubby landlord who looked like a gentle teacher with his metal-rimmed glasses.

'No need to tell us that, Jimmy,' said Christa.

'My name's not Jimmy,' said the landlord, taking the bottle out of the fridge.

'Have you got children?' Birgitt asked as they drank. They drank their last glass and suddenly they weren't tired any more, though the station was now silent and empty and descending into night.

'A daughter. She works in Berlin. And you?'

'No. I had something done when I was young. Here.' She laid her flat hand on her stomach. She was still wearing the summer coat, although the nights were growing cooler now. 'I couldn't after that. Are you a grandmother yet?'

'No, but they're working on it,' she said. 'She's thirty-two. But I was a late mother.'

'Good marriage?'

'My marriage?' She laughed and dismissed the question with a wave of her hand. 'It was a long time ago.'

'I mean your daughter's.'

'Oh, well... they'll make a better job of it. She doesn't come to visit all that often, and I'm always working. Are *you* married, Birgitt?'

'I was. Twice.'

'A double Rittberger.'

'Beg pardon?'

'Oh, just one of those things you say, Birgitt. From figure-skating.'

'Never got into it, Christa. Despite our gorgeous Katharina.'

'In a few years there'll be no-one left who remembers our beautiful Katharina Witt. The great socialist figure-skater.'

They said nothing for a while, drinking sips of their wine and pouring ever smaller amounts from the bottle into their thin, tall glasses and watching the last miniature bottle gradually emptying.

'I don't know if I should look forward to retiring, Christa.'

'Have you got long to go?'

'Not that long. A couple of years.'

'Me too,' she said. 'But you... you still look good. You don't look like... well, you know.'

'Thanks.'

'No, I mean it. You look after yourself, you look good.'

'You do too, Christa.'

'Oh, come off it, I'm a cleaning lady. It's bad for your skin.' She laid her hands on the bar, palms upwards. Her hands were raw and her skin was chapped in several places.

'You're not a cleaning lady,' said Birgitt. She wanted

to put her hand in one of the open palms, but then she left it and stroked the lapels of her summer coat.

'Have you always been on the trains?' she asked.

'Nearly twenty years now,' said Christa. 'That's almost like always – it feels like forever.'

'And before that?'

'Worked in a big hotel, right next to the station, on the west side. Right next to the West concourse. That's where I did my training too. The best hotel in the city, it was.'

'I remember,' said Birgitt. 'They closed it down in the early nineties.'

'Right,' said Christa, 'and I was out of work for a while, then I applied to the railway cleaning services. I don't want to start complaining, it's late.'

'I know what you mean,' said Birgitt. 'Makes you kind of sentimental.'

'And you, how long have you been here, cutting hair by the trains?'

'Feels like forever,' said Birgitt.

'And we never saw each other before?'

'Never mind, we see each other now, that's good enough,' said Birgitt.

'True.' And then they fell silent for a while and drank sips of their cold sparkling wine, which wasn't that cold any more, last sips, and watched the chubby barman who Christa always called Jimmy washing glasses, and other glasses moved to and fro, half-full on the bar, the last movements of the last guests, a ticket inspector drinking coffee, his blue cap with its black peak beside him on the bar. A telephone buzzed in Birgitt's summer coat but she didn't react, took a cigarette out of her pack and lit it.

'Something's buzzing in your pocket,' said Christa.

'No, it's not,' said Birgitt.

'Let's hope it's not your boss again.'

'No, not at this time of night. It's after midnight.'

The telephone fell silent and they sipped at their glasses, and then it started buzzing again and Birgitt took it out of the inside pocket of her summer coat, glanced at the illuminated screen and rejected the call.

'I haven't got a mobile phone,' said Christa, 'because of the radiation.'

'You're kidding me?'

'No, and this way no one can get on my wick at this time of night...'

She wanted to order a small Maria but then she remembered the landlord had already called last orders. She looked at the illuminated screen of Birgitt's phone, which had buzzed again and was still buzzing, and she read some name and looked away quickly before it went out and Birgitt put the phone back in the pocket of her summer coat.

'I feel safer with a phone. Imagine if you got mugged. It's dangerous here at night. Outside, I mean.'

'Yes, it is dangerous. I sometimes walk if I miss the last tram. I steer clear of certain areas, if you know what I mean, but I always have *this* with me.' She reached into the large front pocket of her canvas dungarees and put a can of pepper spray down on the bar next to the miniature bottle. 'If anyone bothers me... and a phone would be no use then, anyway.'

'What if I want to call you?' Birgitt cautiously picked up the pepper spray, holding it in both hands and moving her lips as if reading the writing on the can.

'I've got a landline. But... I might get a mobile for *you*, maybe. There's that big electronics store round the corner here.'

'You really don't have a mobile phone?' Birgitt smiled

52

and put the pepper spray back down on the bar.

'I sometimes think it's not good for us,' said Christa. 'All the air, everything here, everywhere, all the conversations pass through it and the internet and all the signals... It can't be good for our brains.' She tapped her temple with her forefinger and then ran a hand through her hair.

'It's time you went to the hairdresser's, Christa.'

And she leaned against the yellow timetable and looked over at the salon by the staircase leading down to the East concourse, until an old man pulling a huge suitcase on wheels stopped in front of her and then, because she was still looking that way, the crumpled orange safety vest clutched to her chest, he went up close to her and said, 'Excuse me!' And then again, 'Excuse me, please.' She hadn't heard him because he spoke very quietly, but perhaps it was the sounds and the voices of the morning station that swallowed up his voice. She stepped aside and the old man leaned into the timetable, his head almost touching the glass over the yellow paper, he was leaning so far forwards.

She went to one of the bakery stalls that opened at that time of day, at the station end of the platforms, and bought a cardboard cup of coffee. She took off the plastic lid and threw it in the bin next to the stall and blew on the hot drink. She looked up at the big clock above the passage leading to the staircase down to the East concourse. The salon was really busy now. At first, she thought it was the mirrors and she was seeing Birgitt over and over.

But the salon opened in forty minutes' time and it must have been Birgitt's workmates who were arriving now.

She was tired and the coffee wasn't improving matters.

But she wanted to wait until the salon opened. 'Good morning, I'd like a haircut.'

She ran a hand through her hair; it was lank and long and the ends were curling up, stuck together with sweat.

The night before last – so yesterday, no, the day before? – she was a little confused because the days and nights were flowing together more and more... the night before last, she'd taken over the rubbish bins for a few hours. On the trains. She held the rubbish bag under the bin, saw herself in the window pane, bending over the rubbish bin, gripped the metal on either side and pulled and levered until the bin fell towards her, almost empty-ing itself into the big black bag as she held it and shook it so it was really empty before she levered it back into its mounting. And again, she saw herself in the window pane in the yellow of the night lighting, and they touched each other briefly on the shoulders as she walked to the next bin.

'Oh, for God's sake!' She leapt up from her squatting position, let go of the bin as the liquid ran into the black bag, ran over the rubbish bag, dripped onto the floor, onto her legs, darkening the blue of her work trousers, and now the blue fabric was dark and wet on her knees and she smelled the piss running out of the bin. 'Shit, shit, shit!' She stumbled back, held her wet hands away from her body, then dipped them in the bucket of clean-ing water. She wanted to open a sliding window – wasn't there a light there on another train? The inspectors only came rarely, inspected the floor and the windows and the bins with torches, moved almost soundlessly along the trains and between the sidings, popped up and left again.

She held the coffee up so close to her face that she felt the steam hot and damp on her skin and she closed her eyes. She hadn't got in a mess during the night shift just gone but she still wanted to take a shower before she went to see her. Sometimes she changed in the cleaning services building and showered there too.

She was naked and she turned the hot water up until it would go no further. She had put five euros in the slot. Deposit money from the past few days. The big WC Centre with the showers was only a few yards away from the salon. There was a pet shop between the two. She looked at the cages of green and yellow birds sleeping on their perches, the dog collars, food bowls and litter boxes, and she said, 'I've never had a pet. Have you?'

'Two hamsters, when I was little. I've often thought about getting a cat.'

'I don't know. I think then you're really alone.'

'Yes.' They saw each other in the window, standing shoulder to shoulder. Far behind them, a train passed through one of the arches that looked like great gateways, into the night.

She kept pressing the plastic shampoo dispenser and then spread the shampoo over her hair and body. It stung her eyes and she blinked and looked down at herself and sucked in her stomach. Her hair felt soft and good under the water of the shower, and the warm water ran down her back.

'Keep your head still. You have to hold it straight or I'll cut your ear off.' She felt Birgitt's hands on her scalp, heard the quiet snip of the scissors.

She opened her eyes and saw herself in the mirror, a white towel covering her upper body, more and more hair falling onto the fabric. She saw the grey tips, some tufts entirely grey, and she looked in the mirror again, saw Birgitt's hands in her hair, the quiet snip of the scissors moving through her hair with and between the hands. She imagined herself standing outside the shop, watching two women all alone in the salon, one wearing overalls, barely recognizable under the white towel with hair falling onto it, the other behind her, leaning over her, the silver glint of the scissors...

And again she closed her eyes and felt Birgitt's hands and her fingertips on her scalp, and she got goose pimples like she used to when she went to the hairdresser's as a girl. Those touches.

Birgitt laid her hand on hers, felt the chapped, raw skin – 'I'm a working-class heroine' – for a moment it seemed like Christa wanted to pull her hand away but it was just a subtle movement on the wood of the bar.

'Come over with me, I'll cut your hair.'

'What, now, in the middle of the night?'

'Yes. We'll get you back to scratch.'

'It's not that bad, is it?'

'It's bad enough. We'll just go over and I'll cut your hair.'

'If you say so... It'd be nice.'

'My treat.'

'Oh, come off it.'

'No, really.'

'That's sweet of you. You know what, I was outside your salon the other morning...'

'After your night shift? Before my early shift, then.'

'Yes.'

'Why didn't you come in?'

'I don't know. I... I don't know.'

'Probably too many hairdressers in one place for your taste.'

'No, that wasn't it. I'd made sure...'

'Doesn't matter, Christa. It's much nicer now anyway.'

'Yes, it is.'

She sat at the bar and waited, but Birgitt didn't come. She drank a coffee and a small Maria, then she paid the bill and went over to the salon. She could tell there were no lights on from far off. She walked a few minutes past the ends of the platforms but she didn't see Birgitt anywhere. There were a few young lads standing around at the other end, by the late-night minimart and the fast-food outlet.

She went back to the station pub. For a tiny moment she was sure Birgitt would be sitting at the bar and smoking when she came in, but there was no one there and she went back to her coffee and small Maria, sipping at it slowly as she waited.

She ran her hands through her new haircut a few times, through her medium-length hair, and a few times it seemed like she saw tiny silvery tips of hair floating on the air above the bar.

It was a few days ago now that they'd been to the salon in the middle of the night and Birgitt had cut her hair. The shifts had changed over and twice Birgitt had left the light on in the salon, as she'd promised almost as a joke. 'Like a message in a bottle, you know?'

'There's no light on in a bottle, Birgitt.'

'Hmm... Like a message in a bottle with a glowworm in it.'

'You say the craziest things, Birgitt.'

They had arrived after midnight to clean two long-distance trains due to travel again the next morning. And even from far off, Christa had seen the salon's yellow light, though it was only dim, that yellow light of the standing lamp that Birgitt sometimes switched on when she cleaned everything up, turned off the other lights, the last few jobs, put the hair-cutting machines in their chargers, locked all the doors and left the salon.

She'll get in trouble, she thought before she got on the train with the others. But the light was on again the next night, and she smiled as she got on the long-distance train with her broom and cleaning fluids.

The light wasn't on any more, but actually she'd been glad of that – why should Birgitt get in a row with her boss? Still, it would have been nice, a message in a bottle in the dark station concourse. The bar by the staircase was shut at that time too, only a few people standing around over by the West exit at the fast-food outlet, open twenty-four hours.

'And it's only for you. No one else will ever notice.'

She finished her small Maria and paid and left.

She didn't meet Birgitt the next evening either, in the pub by the stairs leading down to the West concourse. Again, she walked a few minutes along the ends of the platforms then went down the escalator, walked through the levels of the big station, briefly considered going to the tunnel linking the platforms, but what was the point?

And again the shifts changed over, days off in between, and she was annoyed at herself for not having a mobile phone. The nights were cold, the first frost came, then it warmed up again slightly. The year was almost over.

She watched the haircutters setting everything up for work. 'I'm a hairdresser, Christa, not a haircutter. Haircutters is what you get at Super Cut.' But Birgitt wasn't one of them. 'Super Cut, what a stupid name...' They laughed. Her fingertips on her scalp. Behind her ears. She leaned against the tiled wall of the shower cubicle, the time was up, the water no longer running, five minutes for five euros, and she took her hand off her stomach and ran it through her wet hair, and water dripped from her hair onto her face.

She had stood outside the building for a good while. Now she climbed the stairs, one at a time. She didn't want to ring the bell at the bottom, didn't know what to say when she heard her voice through the intercom. 'Yes?'

'It's me. Christa, I mean.'

'Yes?'

'I just wanted...' She had stood in front of the doorbell panel for a long time, looking at the names, her hand on the knob of the locked door.

'You're getting sloppy, Ms Fischer.'

'No,' she said, 'yes. It's the night.'

'Well, if you can't...'

'Oh, just shut up, will you?'

She had gone into the salon in the morning after that shift, had changed beforehand in the cleaning services building, hung her overalls up in her locker. She'd brought along her good winter coat but now she was sweating in the far too thick coat, with her orange safety vest over the top. Nasty cold sleet had set in and they were glad to get inside the trains. She had cleaned the windows from inside while the wet flakes smacked against the glass outside, melting and drawing long lines and curves along the panes.

At first the hairdresser wouldn't tell her where Birgitt was and where she lived. Christa only knew which neighbourhood it was. She had taken off the safety vest and put it in her cloth bag. She had gone without her share of the deposit cans and bottles they found on the trains.

'We know each other well, I just...'

'She's off sick. I don't know any more than that.'

'If you had a number or an address...'

'I'm not allowed to just tell you.'

She stood like that for a while in front of the mirrors,

between the hood dryers, while the first customers, men and women, walked past her. She clutched the cloth bag containing the orange safety vest to her chest.

'But Birgitt's my friend, we... I just want to go and visit her.'

The snip of the scissors, the buzz of the hair clippers, and outside the big shop window of the salon the station was awakening, the trains she'd cleaned in the nights before now moving out, through the arches that looked like great gateways.

'Excuse me, excuse me please.' She hadn't heard the boy, even though he was bending over her. She was sitting on the doorstep and the rush-hour traffic was passing on the main road, and perhaps that noise had swallowed up the boy's voice.

And once the boy with a key on a chain around his neck had let her in, she went up the stairs, one at a time. The boy turned around to her a couple of times; he was holding a huge mobile phone in both hands.

He talked into the telephone and she watched him ahead of her before he ran up the staircase.

Then she was outside the door to the flat. Birgitt's name on the doorbell. She stepped up close to the door. She stood like that for a while, listening to the flat. All was quiet. She took a step back, adjusted the lapels of her winter coat, ran a hand through her hair and over her forehead, and then she knocked.

THE BEACH RAILWAY'S LAST RUN

I went to the western breakwater every evening to sit on one of the benches. It was mid-September so the season was coming to an end, but the late summer was sunny and warm and the evenings were long and mild, and plenty of holidaymakers stayed on the beach until it got dark.

At the end of the breakwater was a small lighthouse painted green and white, and behind me too, where the old town met the beach, was another lighthouse, but this one looked much better than the small one; old and very white and very slim, it rose high above the houses of the old town centre. The big lighthouse was also a museum, but it was closed by the time I went to the western break-water in the evening, and the two balconies, one in the middle of the tower and a second one below the top, were abandoned. By day, tourists looked out at the sea from there, and I had stood there once too and looked out at the sea and the ships, twice actually, although there were many years between my two visits to the lighthouse museum. Mind you, *many years* is a bit of an exaggeration, but my second visit had been only a few days earlier.

I took a lot of walks on the beach, sometimes I rented a wicker beach chair and sat for a few hours underneath its blue and white or red and white canopy, reading a book or a newspaper or just looking out at the sea and the ships, sometimes I fell asleep, and I still heard the monotonous calls of the gulls in my dreams, but in the evening I always went to the western breakwater.

Depending on how I sat, I could see the beach from my bench, stretching out to the white Neptune Hotel and further, the yacht harbour, the smaller harbour for the pleasure cruisers and the harbour tours, and of course the lighthouse rising above the houses of the old town centre. But usually I looked out at the open sea or at the waterway called the *großer Strom*, the wide channel, and the many ships putting out to sea from there. I was no expert on maritime matters, I came from the low interior, but the sea air did me good. I wanted to recuperate and I intended to stay in the little town by the sea for a few weeks.

Every few days, accompanied by little tugboats, one of the giant cruise ships moved slowly out of the harbour, along the wide channel to the open sea. Then the tourists would gather on the seafront. And travellers would gather, more crowded and more of them, on the decks of the cruise ship, waving and walking across the decks to the ship's rail, some of them filming as they left the port, and many of the holidaymakers on the seafront filmed the giant ship too, with their cameras or their phones.

One time, I fell asleep on my bench. I must have been very tired, and I didn't wake up until the middle of the night. I put my jacket on; I'd used it to pad out the back of the bench. The small lighthouse at the end of the western breakwater flashed, and the big lighthouse behind me sent its rays out into the night too. I zipped up my jacket and looked out at the sea; I could see the lights of freighters in the distance – there was a city with a container port just along the coast – and I saw the ships on the horizon from my hotel room at night as well.

'There was less water here in the old days,' someone said next to me. I didn't jump, or just a little, because the voice was very quiet. There was someone sitting on another bench, just a yard or two away. I turned to the man but I could barely make him out in the dark, even though the rays of the two lighthouses lit up the night a little, over the western breakwater. He looked like an old man; he had grey or white hair and his voice, too, was old and halting.

'I know it might sound funny when we're here by the sea,' he said. 'But in the old days the wide channel was much narrower, and there was land over there.'

I saw him raise his arm and point to the eastern breakwater. At the end of the eastern breakwater was another small lighthouse. I'd seen it a few times during the day, on my walks.

'You mean over there where the little lighthouse is?' I asked, and scooted closer to the old man on my bench, leaned against the arm rest, and he had moved along to the end of his bench as well so we were sitting closer now.

'The beacon on the eastern breakwater,' the old man corrected me. 'It's not strictly a lighthouse.'

'And it was all land over there?' I didn't understand what he meant or what he wanted, in the middle of the night. I could have just got up and left, I was tired, and at that time of night I'd usually sit on the balcony of my hotel room, drink shots from the minibar and look out at the sky above the sea, which was never quite dark, probably because of the stars... But for some reason I wanted to know what the old man was getting at, what he wanted to tell me. And I was alone in the little town by the sea, no one was waiting for me.

'On the right, behind the eastern breakwater,' the old man said, 'further towards the sea, there's only an island there now, the birds nest there now, but that's where our railway ran in the old days.'

'Our railway,' I repeated, and I saw him nodding.

'We ran directly along the beach and then a little way inland, along the Moorgraben canal – that's still there.'

'So it was like a resort railway,' I said. On my way to the small town I'd passed through Bad Doberan, where they had a steam railway, narrow gauge, that they called the Molly, and it ran between the houses via Heiligendamm and on to the sea.

'No, no,' the old man said, leaning over the arm rest of his bench closer to me, 'not like the Molly. The beach railway. It was our beach railway.'

As the old man said his 'It was our beach railway', the signal light of the large lighthouse illuminated his face for a moment. He really was a very old man with a wrinkled old face, bushy white eyebrows beneath his furrowed brow, but his eyes, as I looked into them in that bright moment as the lighthouse's ray rested on the breakwater and then stretched further and further out to sea and touched the water somewhere out there, his eyes were very alert and young, at least it seemed that way. Later, when I was on the balcony of my room, I thought it might just have been the memory of his youth, or let's say, of the time when he was younger, veritably lighting up his eyes.

He said nothing more, leaning on the arm rest of his bench.

'What kind of beach railway was it?' I asked, because the old man still hadn't said anything and had apparently forgotten me. The breakwater was in semi-darkness again and the sea almost black before us, the lighthouse's signal moving far above us into other parts of the night.

'We ran on electricity,' the old man said just as I was beginning to think he'd nodded off, though his eyes had just been... 'Over there was our depot. Sometimes I think it's at the bottom of the sea now, but they tore it down long ago. Long before they widened the channel. Our beach railway was more like a tram really.'

'A tram by the sea,' I said.

'Yes, a tram by the sea,' he said, and for a moment I

thought I saw him smile.

'No, no,' he said then, suddenly a little louder, and he stood up and sat down again. 'Not a seaside tram, a beach railway.'

'But you're right,' he said a moment later, and again he spoke as quietly as he had a few minutes before, when he'd started talking next to me. 'Some of our old carriages ended up as trams, somewhere, after it was all over here, and I think one of them made it all the way to Nuremberg back then, to the golden West. But we had special carriages too, summer carriages, they were open to the sea.'

'You worked there, on the beach railway I mean?'

'Yes,' he said. 'Where the sea is now, where the bird island is, that's where our depot was, that's where we started from. Always along the beach. Out there where the sea is now.'

'And when... when did it go, your railway?' I don't know why, and I thought about it for a long time on the balcony of my hotel room, where I sat and drank shots from the minibar until the sky gradually turned light and with it the sea, black and grey and dark blue and brighter and brighter... I don't know why but I sensed there was something he wanted to tell me, more than summer carriages open to the sea on the beach railway, there was more to his story than the vanished railway line and the widened channel along which the cruise ships now went out to sea. And sometimes they came back too, cruised along the channel into the port, and then too the decks were packed with people waving and walking around and their heads full of all the foreign countries they'd seen.

'We ran directly along the beach,' the old man said, 'and I was the youngest driver. The Moorgraben's still there. And the guest house on the moor heath is still there too. It's a different house, though. That's where our line ended. We...' He fell silent and stood up but stayed put. 'On the big dune, right near our depot, there was an airfield, the "Luftwaffe Maritime Aviation School". No one remembers that these days.'

He headed back to the old town centre and I went to my hotel. 'I'm always here,' he'd said before he left. 'I come here every evening.'

'Me too,' I wanted to answer, but I didn't know whether it was true, even though I knew I'd see the old man again, him and his beach railway and his story. He vanished behind the lighthouse, somewhere in the narrow streets of the old town centre. And as the sun came up later, as I was sitting in an armchair I'd pushed out onto the balcony from my hotel room, I tried to spot the bird island, saw the lighthouse in front of the houses of the old town centre and the beacons on the breakwaters, and I fell asleep.

And in my dream I was in the beach railway's summer carriage, something I'd never heard of before that day... Seagulls flapped around the open summer carriage, eyes alert for leftovers, a few children threw bits of bread up in the air and laughed when the gulls squabbled mid-flight, and then I was suddenly standing at a stop, couldn't remember getting off but that's how it is in dreams sometimes, and the beach railway ran past me, and for a moment I saw the old man in the driver's cab behind his cranks and levers, and beside him a little boy and a girl, both leaning against him, but before I could take a closer look the train simply ran into the waves – the tracks led into the sea.

'Who wants to remember it anyway?' the old man said. 'It was all gone after the war.'

We were sitting at the foot of the western break-water again. I'd never noticed the old man until the night before.

But I'd had other things on my mind. I'd come to the little town by the sea to recuperate, to forget all the crap I'd left behind me.

'Did it get bombed, then, the railway?' I asked. It was still light but the sea was beginning to turn red, a few holidaymakers packing their blankets and things together down on the beach. The old man was wearing a scruffy leather jacket, the kind named after the communist Ernst Thälmann, back in the day.

'Bombed?' The old man looked at me, apparently thinking about the question. 'No,' he said. 'Apart from that one hit...' He nodded, ran a hand over his face and then through his white, short-cropped hair.

'So why...'

'The Russians dismantled it all. And who needed a beach railway in those tough times?'

'How old were you back then?' I asked, and then I added a quick, 'If you don't mind me asking...'

'You're a polite young man,' the old man said, and I saw him smile. 'You should be asking how old I am now...'

'I'm forty-two,' I said, 'and I don't feel all that young right now. You must have been a child then, what... sixty-five, sixty-six years ago.'

'Thank you,' the old man said. 'But I was a young man back then, young man. Seventeen years old. That was old enough, '44 and '45, old enough to... But someone had to drive the train. The men had all been sent to the front and I got promoted from apprentice to train driver. Usually we were only taking soldiers to the maritime aviation school. Or from the maritime aviation school to the guest house. Not many holidaymakers back then. And the winter never ended. It may sound funny but it was the happiest time of my life.'

'Even though there was a war on?'

'Yes, even though there was a war on, young man,' he said, and I was instantly ashamed of my question. What did I know? But I had the feeling I had to ask him so he'd go on talking, so he'd go on with the story he'd begun the night before.

'Because you got promoted?'

'Ach, it wasn't much of a promotion. I just drove the train, that's all. Our beach railway. And my young cousin got a ticket inspector's uniform and clipped the tickets. Little Karli...'

'Nice name.'

'Yes. His real name was Karlmann but we only ever called him Karli. You know what's funny? I often think it was summer back then, all the weeks we ran the beach railway together, Karli, me... and *her*. Late summer, like now.'

The old man drew a deep breath, as though he could smell his late summer.

'The girl,' I said.

'Yes, the girl,' he said. The sun was setting now, the sea and the banks of clouds now red. I had looked out at that ever-darkening red these past evenings, and perhaps that was why I hadn't noticed the old man on the next bench along.

'She came with the refugees from the East.' The old man started back into his story.

I don't know how long we'd simply sat there in silence and looked out at the sea and the sky, and suddenly I was no longer sure when he'd first mentioned the girl in his story. They were on the beach railway, the sky glowing red in the East, but it wasn't the sunset. His young cousin Karli walked through the almost-empty carriages of the beach railway in his inspector's uniform, far too big for him, the old man sat in the driver's cab and turned the big cranks and levers, and she sat behind him and looked over his shoulder at the tracks ahead of them. Winter and snow and a sky above the sea like in late summer.

'She came with the refugees from the East. Without her parents. I never asked her what had happened along the way. She lived at Karli's house – Karli brought her along one day.'

'How old was Karli?'

'Hmm, let me think... eleven or twelve. I think Karli was twelve at the time. Yes. His parents had a farm outside of town. They housed refugees with them.'

'And how old was *she*?'

'She was the same age as me. Our birthdays were even in the same month.'

I wanted to ask him which month, but then I didn't.

'And all this was just before the end of the war?'

'Yes. No. The war went on a lot longer. Those last months were very long. First the men disappeared and they let me drive our beach railway. And my little Karli was the inspector. Then came the refugees from the East. And she came with the refugees.'

And I wanted to ask the old man what her name was, but I knew I mustn't ask, knew I had to wait until he said her name.

'I liked Karli a lot. I don't have any brothers and sisters. My father died before the war, and Karli's father was my father's brother. And he was like my little brother. Yes, he was.'

The big lighthouse rising above the houses of the old town centre began now to send its light out into the ever-darker evening, into the night. And the two beacons flashed as well, one ahead of us, at the end of the western breakwater, the other beacon on the eastern breakwater visible far across the water, where the beach railway had once run. The old man took a tied-up pouch out of one pocket in his Thälmann jacket and opened it. He took out a sheet of cigarette paper, rested it on his leg and crumbled a little tobacco from the leather pouch onto the paper. But a slight wind blew up so he didn't manage to roll his cigarette. Once he'd tried it a few times, I stood up and said, 'I can do that for you, if you like.'

'That's very kind of you, young man,' he said, and I took the tobacco and the paper and turned my back to the wind and rolled him a cigarette. And while I was rolling I did some thinking and worked out how old he must be now, if he'd been seventeen back then in '44, '45. No, he didn't look that ancient, but we only ever saw each other in the rays of the lighthouses and the light of the waning day. The tobacco in the leather pouch was dry and very crumbly. He probably only smoked very rarely; I'd never seen him smoking before, but then we'd only known each other one evening and one night.

I handed him the cigarette and he took a large metal lighter from one of his jacket pockets. The flame illuminated his face. I saw that the lighter's metal was rusty. He coughed.

'We used to sit in my driver's cab together and smoke, the tracks ahead of us. We'd usually share a cigarette; she'd put it between my lips – I had to drive the train. All of us used to smoke at seventeen. And the winter never ended but it's late summer again in my memory. I used to call her Ladybertha. Like the insect, you know, one of those ladybirds, a ladybertha.'

70

'I've never heard them called that – ladybertha.'

'No, it was just a pet name. Ladybird, ladybird, fly away home...' He sang those last words, quietly humming a tune. 'Ladybird, fly away home... Her name was Bertha. She came to town with one of the groups of refugees, came walking all the way from the East.'

And as I sat on the balcony of my hotel room later on, I tried to imagine her, his Ladybertha, the way he'd told me about her.

'She had shoulder-length dark hair. Brown. And my God, could she run like the wind. When we were on the beach – there must have been snow on the ground – she was always in the lead. I could hardly keep up. She wasn't very tall but I was much taller then than I am now, believe you me. Sometimes she had two plaits; I liked that. Her plaits. What do you call those tassels? At the bottom of plaits. I held them like a paintbrush and brushed her face with them. Tickled her nose to make her laugh. I often remember her nose. That probably sounds funny. But I'm an old man.'

'No, it doesn't sound funny.'

'She had a thin nose, slightly bent, a bit to the left, just a tiny bit, how can I put it...?'

I saw him move his hand slowly and carefully in mid-air, a little way in front of his face. The cigarette I'd rolled for him was in his other hand; it had gone out but he didn't seem to notice. He wasn't trying to smoke it any more and he soon simply dropped it on the ground.

'She could put on this very firm look, she'd frown and wrinkle her nose and screw up her eyes, but when she laughed... She didn't laugh often but Karli always made her laugh. That was good. He was a real joker. Always on the train in his uniform, much too big for him. The soldiers, the trainee pilots, they all liked him. Used to give him chocolate and we'd share it. In the depot or on the beach. There must have been a lot of snow back then. And my God, could she run. We'd usually outrun Karli. On the beach, in the snow. He'd get angry at that. After he'd got us so many cigarettes, from the soldiers. For Bertha and me. He could talk the soldiers, the trainee pilots, into giving him anything. No one could ever be angry with him.'

And I looked out from my balcony over the snow-covered beach, saw little Karlmann between the white dunes, and far away the young old man with his Ladybertha, nothing but two black dots against the white of the snow, against the grey of the sea.

I went back into the room and called my wife. I often called her at night, when I'd drunk shots from the minibar, listened to her voice over and over on her answer-phone. Every time I called, I knew she wouldn't pick up.

And then my telephone buzzed on the breakwater; I'd folded up my jacket again and put it between my back and the bench.

'What's that?' the old man asked.

'Someone's calling me,' I said.

'Here?' the old man asked, amazed, and then he seemed to remember what year it was, and he asked, 'Don't you want to answer it?'

'No,' I said. 'Not really.'

'Sometimes I imagine what it would have been like if we could have done that back then,' said the old man. 'Just call each other up. No matter how far away you are. No matter what's happened.'

'It doesn't work now, either,' I said, feeling the phone fall silent against my back. I didn't check who'd called until I got to my hotel room. But it was just an old friend. No one knew I was up on the coast.

I always left the balcony door open when I went to bed. I fell asleep faster when I could hear the sea.

And again, the beach railway ran through my dreams. The overhead wire had frozen and flashes of electric lightning crackled between the wire and the current collector on the roof of the train. The three of them were in the empty carriages. Karli, the old man and *her*. The funny thing was, he always stayed old in my dream. He looked a little taller, stronger, but his face was old. They were riding in the open summer carriage, and the wind whistled cold between us. I was there now too, on the beach railway, not seeing them from outside any more, the way you can watch and see everything in dreams, like you're everywhere. I had got on at one of the stops, a stop sign with a timetable in the sand of the beach, and now I was sitting at the very back of the carriage, watching the three of them. *She* sometimes sat behind him and then beside him in the driver's cab, and little Karlmann ran along the carriage, the sleeves of his uniform rolled up, far too big, making jokes and comments and laughing at them uninterrupted. Cigarettes and chocolate. He winked at me from beneath the blue peak of his cap – 'Tickets please, let's see your tickets, please!' – and then he walked along the beach railway carriage and pretended he couldn't see from underneath his cap and kept bumping into every seat, and then he stumbled again and I could hear him laughing.

'And do you know why I remember it so well?'

'Remember what, exactly?' I asked. We were back at the breakwater, or were we still there? It was drizzling, the sky was full of clouds, racing in clumps and wild formations over the sea, although I could hardly feel the wind where I was. The clouds kept tearing apart, and then we saw the sunset. No, the sunset was long gone, but its light still rested beneath the darkness. And yellow and red lights from ships beneath the clouds, far out at sea, sometimes here and sometimes there and then somewhere else.

'That her nose that had a slight bend to the left...'

'Because you...'

'Because that's where her heart was,' the old man said. 'You can feel something like that and see it beating. If you... This must sound funny to you...'

'No, it doesn't.'

'...as if that slight bend to the left was pointing to it. To her left breast. Can you remember your wife's nose now, right this moment? And how her heart beats... Can you feel it? And do you remember all those little things?'

'No,' I wanted to say. 'I don't know,' I wanted to say, but I didn't reply.

'I'm sorry,' the old man said, and his voice grew quieter and calmer again, 'I'm getting silly and sentimental.'

'I would be too,' I said. 'After all those years.'

The old man nodded. And it was only then that I saw he was holding the rusty lighter in his left hand. He flicked the lid up and down again, on and off, but it must have got wet in the drizzling rain that had set in a few minutes ago.

'My cousin Karli brought her along,' he said. 'She was suddenly there.' But I knew that already.

He had become more taciturn on our third evening. Before he'd talked about her nose and his thoughts about her nose and his memories of her nose and her plaits, we'd sat silently on our benches for a long time.

We'd turned up the collars of our jackets, the leather of his dark-brown Thälmann jacket shiny from the rain, but then the rain let off and in the end it stopped altogether.

'What are you doing here by the sea, anyway?' he asked, the lighter still in his hand, and it sounded like he was re-emerging very slowly from his past, from those last runs on his beach railway.

'Just a bit of a holiday,' I said.

'I've told you a lot, haven't I?'

'You have,' I said. 'About a ladybird.'

And when I dreamed of the beach railway at night the balcony door was open as usual, and before I fell asleep I'd listened to my wife's voice on her answerphone. I missed her so much. We were all on the beach railway in the middle of the refugees walking, walking miles and miles like he'd told me, but they seemed not to notice us at all, perhaps because we were heading in the direction they came from, men, women, children, so many children, on horse-drawn carts, hand carts, on foot, the beach railway that looked like an electric tram heading in the opposite direction, and the old man in the driver's cab turning the big cranks and levers, her standing next to him, pressing up to him, holding onto his shoulder as she watched the streams of people fleeing, the people she'd arrived with herself, and little Karlmann in his inspector's uniform looked silently out of the window at the back of the carriage, while the refugees trudged through the snow towards the town and it snowed and snowed, on and on, the sea grey and floes of ice floating on the water. And the carts the children and old women were sitting on, in amongst chests of drawers and household goods, left tracks in the snow that looked like train tracks leading away from our train tracks, until they were covered up again by the falling snow, and I sat on the beach train, put my arm around my wife, I wanted to put my arm around her but the seat next to me was empty. And through the frosted windows, I saw a boy and a girl running along the beach, pelting each other with snowballs.

'How she could walk,' the old man said. 'I could barely keep up when we went walking on the beach and she suddenly started marching, straight ahead – I had to run to catch up with her. We fell down in the snow, we lay in the snow, we hugged in the snow. And warmed up in our beach railway depot; there was a little iron stove there. My little Karli was grinning right across his face, but he left us alone. Once I fell asleep in the depot, we had a camp bed there by the stove where we used to rest, and once I fell asleep in the camp bed. And when I woke up again she was standing over me and she said: You look like a dead body – they hunch up like that as well. And I didn't ask how she knew that; I'd never seen a dead body close up, even though the bombs were falling and the frontline was getting closer every day. I drove our beach railway. And she'd always sit in the cab beside me. I wanted her to stay, I wanted to be with her all the time.'

He stopped talking and nodded his head a few times; was he trembling? He was a very old man, coughing as he smoked a cigarette I'd rolled for him.

'And her parents, or any other relatives?' I asked.

'She was all alone in the world. You say that so easily, but that's how it was in those days. All alone... the world.'

And again, I looked out of the window of the beach railway and there were bodies lying in the snow, and gulls were perching on them and pecking at the frozen flesh.

The old man was sitting behind the big hand crank in the driver's cab as always, but apart from him and me, there was no one else in the carriage this time. Ships drifted on the sea between the ice floes and swarms of seagulls flapped screaming around the ships, plunging over and over onto the decks. Where was Karli, and where was *she*? Slowly, very slowly I walked along the empty carriage to the driver's cab and saw over the old man's shoulder that we were heading directly into a huge flame. Was it the aviation school he'd told me about? 'Stop,' I called out, 'for God's sake, stop!' But he seemed not to hear me, turning and turning the crank, and the front carriage of the little beach railway raced screeching along the tracks, and the snow flew up on either side.

And then he did turn around to me, his face strangely grey and soot-smudged as though we'd already been in the midst of the flames we were heading towards, and he moved his lips – but I couldn't understand him because a loud buzz like from engines had set in, no, it wasn't seagulls out there, it was planes, countless planes. And I lowered my head right close to his mouth so that his lips almost touched my ear. 'He's dead – I killed him.'

'Who?' I shouted against the noise, and then the flames swallowed us up, yes, they swallowed us whole, a wall of flames that we vanished into, and I felt us all being torn to pieces by an explosion, and I was so frightened of the darkness and death, and then I woke up.

It was a clear, sunny day when I went out on the balcony, but the summer would soon be over. It was nearly time for me to go back home. But no one was waiting for me there, and I was on leave for the foreseeable future. 'We'd recommend you take a break, go to the seaside.'

'Why the seaside? How do you know we...'

I clutched my phone on the balcony and my eyes wandered along the beach, where fewer and fewer bathers showed up with every passing day. The night before, I hadn't called my wife's number to hear her voice on the answerphone.

The hotel was a little way above the beach. From my

balcony, I could see the little town and the harbour and the breakwaters with the beacons. The corner room with its panoramic view was costing me the last of my savings, but we'd spent a few days here back then, after our wedding.

How many years ago was that? I'd lost all sense of time since I'd been sitting by the breakwater with the old man in the evenings.

I was tired and wrecked by the night and the dreams and still I spent all day walking, walked several kilometres along the beach, getting further and further from the route of the vanished beach railway and then going back again after all, taking one of the pleasure boats that carried the tourists along the wide channel and around the harbour. We passed close by the bird island, more of a large dune, and went out to sea, always sticking close to the headland though. That was where it had once run, his beach railway, and the aviation school and the depot were somewhere; I stood by the rail and looked down at the waves.

We continued to the Moorheide, where there was a pier where a few people disembarked, and the boat went on into the Heidegraben, a canal leading a little way inland. I spotted the restaurant from far off. It was an old building with a thatched roof. Hadn't he said the old tavern had gone, along with the waiting hall where the holidaymakers used to sit? But they'd been all alone there that winter. The boat moored and we got off and sat on benches and chairs on the terrace, ate and drank and waited for the boat to set off again.

'Departure in five minutes and twenty-four seconds,' shouted Karlmann, who everyone only ever called Karli, running between the tables and benches on the terrace. We could hear him laughing, his inspector's cap far too low over his face, and he pushed the red peak of the cap up with his signalling disc as he leaned down to me. 'A ticket, sir, for our special trip? You have to go back, don't you?'

'Two,' I said. 'For me and my wife.' A bell rang somewhere.

'No,' the old man said that evening, 'it's all gone, the restaurant, the waiting hall, it went long ago, along with the railway.'

'But I went there today,' I said.

'It's all gone,' said the old man. 'Just like *she* went, back then.'

'Where to?'

'She just left. Probably over to the American zone. No one knew exactly. Late May, early June. It was a lovely May, a sudden summer. We'd been bathing, for the first time. The next day, she was gone.'

'The Russians?' I asked.

'I always looked after her, always looked out for her. She shouldn't have gone, not after the thing with Karli. No, she shouldn't have left.'

'What happened to Karli?' I asked. With the beacons on the breakwater and the flashes of the big lighthouse behind us illuminating our faces, we were sitting next to each other on one bench that evening, that night. I'd brought along a few miniature bottles from the minibar in the panorama corner room and balanced them on the wooden slats between us. That morning I'd seen one of the giant cruise ships setting off, its decks crowded with waving travellers; now the wide channel was motionless before us, but the signal rays alighted over and over on the almost black surface of the water.

'Karli,' he said and then stopped for a few seconds, and I could hear him breathing, the bottles clinking quietly as he reached for them. 'I could have saved him. But I was alone, and I was seventeen.' He held one of the bottles in his hand, trying to open the lid but failing. I took it from him, opened it and handed it back to him. For a moment he looked like he wanted to drink but then he threw the bottle out into the darkness.

'I fetched Bertha out of the overturned carriage and carried her down to the beach. Karli was trapped. He was lying outside and his leg was trapped, I... He looked at me as I fetched her out of the carriage. I still see it now, him looking at me. Please help me. He was crying. I liked him so much, my cousin Karli. I should have pulled him out, I should have tried.'

He looked at me. What could I have said?

'But I rescued *her* from the overturned front carriage. And when I came back... He was crying when I carried her down to the beach. Don't go, he called out. But I had to get her away from there before I could help him. I was alone. The whole sky was dark red. I wanted to rescue him but when I came back...'

I drank the last corn schnapps or vodka and threw the bottle out into the dark. I heard it hit the water, just a quiet splash like when you throw a small stone into the sea, or a snowball in winter.

We sat side by side for a long time, looking out at the water. He was holding the metal lighter again. Hadn't he told me *she* had given it to him? An old soldier's lighter. She'd found it somewhere on her long walk from the East, before she found him and his beach railway and then flew away again like a ladybertha, like a ladybird.

It was drizzling when I went back to the western breakwater a few days later. The old man was sitting on a bench, and I sat down on the bench next to him. He seemed not to notice me, but when I'd... how long ago was it now...? when I'd come to the breakwater the first time, I hadn't seen him right away either.

'There was less water here in the old days,' said the old man after a while, not looking at me.

'I know,' I said, and I got up again and walked back to the hotel through the rain.

TWO

My old friend R.'s father was sitting on the balcony. He looked very small and thin in the big armchair R. and his mother had put out there for him. There was a green blanket over his legs, the days had grown cool, and the chair felt clammy when I put my hand on the padded back. R.'s father looked up at me briefly and nodded. He whispered something but all I could understand was the word 'nice'.

We stood next to him by the railing and looked out at the low-rise concrete blocks of the estate on the edge of town, behind it the large industrial parks, and far off we saw the white ribbon of the motorway, its hum audible at night.

R. helped his father out of the chair and then we grabbed one arm each and helped him walk slowly to the front door. He was wearing a dressing gown over his tracksuit, and I could feel the tubes and the bag when I put my arm under his. We took him to my car.

We drove across town, R. sitting behind me, leaned up against the back of my seat and watching his father, who was in the passenger seat, his head resting against the window. The glass fogged up, a misty white spot next to his mouth. He'd wanted so much to take one last ride around his old neighbourhood but now it looked like he was asleep.

As we passed a fairground, he raised his head and pointed at the rides and stalls. It was autumn and the last of the fairground people were working their way through the villages into the town. I stopped the car. R. went to one of the stalls and got a plastic cup of beer for his father. He took a few mouthfuls, coughed and leant against the car and pointed at the Ferris wheel rising above the stalls and the carousels on the other side of the fair. I looked at R. and he nodded, and his father put his arms over our shoulders, and we walked very slowly along the narrow alleys of shooting ranges and food stalls and rides until we got to the big wheel. The fair wasn't busy, even though it was getting dark.

We sat in the swaying passenger car and looked out over the fair and the houses and the flat expanse outside of town. R.'s father was trying to tell us something but we couldn't understand his whispers; the wind was whistling around us and the music from the stalls and the rides came blaring up from below. But then we saw what he meant. The wind turbines. We could see them clearly from up there. There were hundreds of them erected on the flat expanse outside the town, a forest of wind turbines, and as dusk set in, the red warning lights below the rotors began to light up. R.'s father had been a metalworker, he'd spent the last twenty years on the floor of a big production hall, crawling inside steel towers for wind turbines, welding them together. Until the illness.

The big wheel had stopped turning, and the cars swung and swayed, and we stared out at the winking red lights and the rotors gradually vanishing in the darkness, which seemed very close, and my old friend R.'s father raised his hand for a second.

THE CRACK

As he passed through the stairwell to his ground-floor flat that night, he instantly sensed something wasn't right.

He stood by the letterboxes as usual and looked for the letterbox key among the others on his keyring, but then he stopped and listened; it was quiet in the building and the street outside wasn't busy at that time either.

Standing by the row of letterboxes, he couldn't yet see the entrance to his flat, but perhaps he'd felt the draught, he thought later, or he'd heard the front door, ajar, bumping in the draught.

He stood outside his flat, his briefcase down on the floor, and looked at the slightly open door until the light in the stairwell switched off automatically.

He turned it on again, took his briefcase in both hands and pressed it against the wood of the door until the door opened slowly. He peered into the dark hallway.

He couldn't spot anything on the doorframe, no broken-off wood; it looked like someone had opened his flat using a key. He stepped onto the threshold – the slight creak he knew so well; he'd been living in the flat for almost fifteen years, since he'd moved out of his mother's place – and the moment he switched the light on he saw that his cowboy boots were missing. He kept them on the top shelf of his shoe rack, he'd bought them on holiday in America a few years back, the best leather, hand-made with silver details on the shaft, but now they were gone.

He leaned his briefcase against the shoe rack, went back out to the stairwell, double-locked the outside door and went up to the first floor, cautious not to make too much noise. No one lived there; there was only one flat directly above his, and he tiptoed further up to the second floor. The two doors there seemed to be intact, light shining behind their barred windows. He heard a TV show coming from one of the flats, the sound blaring louder when the adverts started, and he turned back. As he reached the last landing the light switched off and he saw the bright crack through which the light of his flat, his hallway, fell into the dark stairwell.

He examined the lock. It wouldn't lock any more. His key still went in and he could turn it, but the bit of the key met no resistance any more; the lock rattled back and forth with the key in it.

He pulled the door closed anyway, and then he began to examine the rooms. Something had stopped him from doing so up until then, as though he were scared to find his flat changed.

He opened the kitchen door; his bike, usually in front of the kitchen cupboards, was gone. He always took it inside the flat because he was worried it might get stolen from the basement. He often cycled to work, his briefcase on the luggage rack, but it had rained the past two days and he'd taken the bus.

Then he saw that his little kitchen radio was missing. It had been a good little kitchen radio, with a digital clock and an egg-timer function, a present from his mother years ago. Grundig, a good company. He still didn't understand why someone would steal his kitchen radio, though. What was it worth? It was more than ten years old, one of the last things his mother had given him.

He reached for a knife in the sink, a long, pointed bread knife, but then he left it. What would be the point – the flat was empty. Though he hadn't yet checked all the rooms. He picked up the knife. Put it down again. He took his phone out of his inside pocket, dialled the emergency services, put it on loudspeaker and hung up again when the first long note of the ringing tone rang out in his kitchen. He noticed how dry his mouth was, and he picked up a glass and filled it under the tap.

He walked slowly into the other rooms. They'd been there, as well. His stereo was missing from the living room. His desk drawers had been opened and searched. The small flatscreen TV had gone. Nothing seemed to be missing in the bedroom, but his bed, made that morning as ever, was messed up. What the hell had they been doing in his bed? He opened the drawer of his bedside table. The lamp on the marble top dazzled him and he turned the green shade downwards. They had flicked through the photo album he kept in the drawer. It was still half-open with one page bent, and a photo was missing.

In the light of his bedside lamp, he saw himself sitting on his mother's lap as a little child, black and white. He turned the pages, his last girlfriend on the beach, how gorgeous she was, and while he was still turning the pages, he pushed the drawer closed with the other hand, let go of the album and sat down on the bed. The drawer was still open; he saw his baby foot on his mother's knee, the photo was missing, only the black mounting corners glued to the page between the other photos. The drawer had got stuck and he pressed against the wood and then the marble top slid, only balanced loosely on top, so he let go of the drawer, which still wouldn't quite close, pushed the marble top back into place and looked at the messed-up bed he was sitting on. He got up. He went into the bathroom. They didn't seem to have been in there. Everything was in its right place. He sat down on the closed toilet lid. The newspapers on the window-sill. He remembered reading something about a series of break-ins. Organized gangs. He sat on the toilet lid and looked at himself in the mirror above the sink.

After a while, minutes or hours, he got up and lay down on the sofa in the living room. He was cold and he pulled the blanket over himself, which he kept rolled up like a cushion at one end. The blanket smelled strangely sweet. Had they sat on his sofa as well? Then he got up again and pushed the shoe rack in front of the door to his flat. His briefcase, previously leaning against the shoe rack, was now in the middle of the hall. He looked at it for a while from the living-room doorway, then he went back for it and put it down next to him by the sofa. He lay awake for a long time, staring at the ceiling and looking into the darkness of his closed eyelids, and he listened to the flat and listened to the building while the early-morning traffic set in outside on the street.

Late in the morning he got up, having barely slept. He had to go to work in a few hours' time. It was a nice autumn day outside, he could tell through the slats of the blind, but he'd have to take the bus. The office of the courier service where he took care of order processing was outside of town, in an industrial park. He had to walk another ten or fifteen minutes from the bus stop. He smelled the autumn fires at night. There was always someone burning wood or leaves in the allotments and the gardens around the industrial park at that time of year.

'Did you call the police?'

'Yes. Yes.'

'Because of the insurance, I mean.'

'Yes, of course.'

'Otherwise the insurance won't pay.'

'There was nothing missing – I surprised them. They ran away. It's just the door.'

'Yes, the door. The police have to make a note of the damages, then you can go to the insurance company...'

Why couldn't the man from the locksmith's just be quiet and change the lock? He was standing in his hallway, the doors to all the rooms closed, watching the locksmith squatting on the threshold and applying various tools to the lock and the doorframe by turn.

'If you're lucky something might turn up again... but usually it's gone. I wouldn't get my hopes up...'

'There's nothing missing,' he said again, but the locksmith just went on talking. 'You're not the first, they've been all round this neighbourhood, all round town. Foreigners, if you ask me, Yugos, Turks, you know.'

'I told you... They were surprised breaking in. Didn't even get inside the flat.'

That morning, after he'd got up, he'd stood in the bedroom doorway for a while, looking at his messed-up bed and the wonky bedside table with the drawer still open, inside it his photo album that they'd looked at. Then he'd closed the door.

He'd gone into the bathroom and lifted up the toilet lid and the toilet seat.

He usually peed standing up, even though his last girlfriend had talked him into sitting down. The reason was simply that he didn't believe he could fully empty his bladder sitting down, for anatomical reasons. Why had she left him, anyway? All that arguing over a car, why he didn't want to move in with her, and so on.

He stood facing the toilet and looked down at the pale-yellow water. Someone hadn't flushed. He tried to remember when he'd last used the toilet.

He had come home, found the door ajar, he had searched his flat, a lot of things were missing, and he'd discovered they'd looked at his photos or at least flicked through them, he'd sat down on the closed toilet lid, he'd lain down on the sofa...

On the bus, he clutched his new keys, still thinking about whether they'd used his toilet. The urine didn't smell like his. He had flushed it away, kept pressing the flush until no more water came.

And then he was back on a bus, just after ten in the evening. The briefcase with his laptop in it between his feet. His eyes were burning; he'd spent the last few hours staring at the screen and accepting orders and printing out routes and writing invoices and forwarding the processed orders. He closed his eyes. The black girl courier had joked around with him again. Did she fancy him? She was single, as far as he knew, and they got along well, and she often stood up close to him when they talked, so close he'd thought about just kissing her a couple of times. Sometimes he thought about her when he masturbated. And she'd joked around with him as usual but this time he hadn't played along, just stared at the screen, at the numbers and data.

When he woke up, he realized he'd gone too far. It took him a couple of seconds to remember he was on the bus, on the way back from work. In that brief sleep between stops he had dreamed there were policemen in his flat, combing through room after room. 'No,' he'd called out, 'you can't go in there,' but they'd searched through his things, flicked through his photos, simply refusing to leave.

He stood on the other side of the road and looked over at the dark windows of his ground-floor flat. He had got off the bus at the bridge over the train tracks, and had walked all the way back to his house.

He had stood on the bridge before he started walking, and had looked down at the branching web of train tracks. Buildings stood on either side of the route, their walls falling steeply to the embankment, looking like cliffs in the night.

Why he wandered back towards the bridge later on, he couldn't say. Didn't think about it either.

He had been looking at the windows of his ground-floor flat for a few minutes, clutching his new keys. He turned around. Walked along the road, away from his flat, away from his building. A bus drove past him, its seats empty, only one man at the very back, by the big rear window, apparently asleep. His head was resting on his chest, swaying slightly to the rhythm of the road.

He drank a beer in a corner pub where he used to go occasionally, but that must have been ten or fifteen years back in his early twenties, and he was surprised the pub still existed. There used to be a tram stop right outside the pub but the line had been closed down for a while now; they'd even tarred over the tram tracks. The place was pretty empty and the landlord said, 'Just the one beer, though, we're closing,' and he put his briefcase on the bar stool next to him and drank his beer and left.

He thought about his bed as he walked along the tarred tracks, his bed that he'd found messed up, thought about his photos that they'd touched... What had they been expecting between the pages and the pictures? Money? Share certificates? Credit cards? Or were they surprised and touched by the traces of his life? Looked into his memories... Stole one of his memories.

He'd rarely looked at the album before he went to sleep. But he knew it was there, in his bedside drawer.

He walked along the road parallel to the train tracks, underneath the bridge he'd stood on earlier, and he had the feeling a flash blinded him from every kebab shop, from every amusement arcade, from every bar, like someone was photographing him.

It was probably the beer and the vodka. He didn't usually drink a lot and he couldn't take much alcohol. But then he saw he had a bottle of fizzy apple juice and a coffee. He was at a kebab shop, leaning on the counter, voices behind him. He'd stopped drinking after that one beer in the corner pub by the tram stop where no trams stopped any more.

'Organized gangs,' he'd read in the paper, 'Foreigners, Yugos, Turks, you know,' the man from the locksmith's had said. Four black mounting corners, no longer holding a photo in among all the other photos.

He heard the voices behind him, foreign languages, all different languages, voices, languages that sounded to him like cawing, big dark birds flapping and cawing along the wide road after him, but he didn't turn around and he leaned on the counter, one arm on his briefcase, while he drank his coffee and sipped at the apple juice now and then.

He imagined he'd attached his briefcase to his wrist with a handcuff, one steel ring around the handle, the other around his arm.

How else could he have not lost his briefcase on his escape?

He was running. What had happened? He was running. And they were coming after him.

He hadn't been down that road for years. Amusement arcades, betting shops, kebab shops, internet cafés, second-hand shops, Arabic-looking tea rooms with curly letters above the entrance... Two thin girls had come towards him as he turned onto the street. Then he saw that one of the girls was a thin boy. They looked pale and they stared at him out of big, hungry eyes. Junkies, crystal freaks who wanted to steal his briefcase.

He hadn't been down that road for years, even though it was only a few bus stops away from his house. There used to be a cinema there – was it the Wintergarten or was it the 'Friendship Cinema'? – he'd watched fairy-tale films there with his mother when he was very young.

When he'd got off the bus at the bridge and walked back the stops he'd gone too far, he had crossed the wide road with the railway tracks running along the backs of its houses. What the hell is going on here, he'd thought.

Explosions of lights from amusement arcades with their doors wide open, a green verge along the side of the road, figures on the benches staring at him; he ran. Why was he running?

And while he was running he saw, out of the corner of his eye, a lit-up cabin, next to the pavement, it looked like a parking attendant's cabin, walls made of glass, figures behind the glass, uniforms looking out into the night, the green-and-white letters POLICE up on the roof of the cabin.

Why hadn't he run to them, he asked himself later, sitting on the staircase in the old derelict house. A kind of outpost. Organized gangs. 'Yugos, Turks,' he shouted into the stairwell. Before, he had stood outside one of the second-hand places and thought he'd seen his bike at the back of the shop. In between other bikes. He'd seen the two thin junkies reflected in the window, he walked on and they vanished again, and other shapes appeared and crowded him... followed him...

'Is that you, my boy?'

He jumped. He must have fallen asleep for a moment. The light was on in the stairwell and an old woman was standing over him. She was wearing a net of some kind over her hair and blinking at him through a big pair of tinted glasses. He hadn't thought anyone still lived in the old derelict building. He had run to the house on the corner, still hearing footsteps behind him; the door next to a big, empty shop window was open a tiny crack, he could tell as he ran past; he stopped, grabbed the handle and pushed it down; the door wasn't easy to open, probably warped and jammed, but he inserted one hand into the crack and pressed and shouldered the wood until the door opened, and he stepped quickly into the dark shop and pulled it closed behind him.

The light of the streetlamps fell through the dirty pane, and he took a couple of steps into the room so they wouldn't see him from the street, and then he found another door, that one not locked either, and he found himself in a big, dark stairwell.

He almost bumped into the wooden pillar where the staircase began, where the wooden banister started its curve; he could feel the carvings, the decorations, as he reached for the pillar. Then he walked up slowly, one hand on the banister, the old stairs creaking so loudly he was afraid for a moment his pursuers might hear him from outside on the street...

'Is that you, my boy?' He stood up, and the old woman standing bent, two steps above him, looked him in the face and reached a hand out towards him. 'I knew I heard someone coming in downstairs.' She was wearing a black coat, open at the front, and he made out a stained grey nightshirt under the black fabric.

She touched his face with her fingertips and he wanted to pull back, but then he didn't and he felt her cracked fingernails on his skin. She smelled strongly of talc, lavender or something like that, beneath it the scent of her body, and for an instant he remembered opening the toilet lid in his flat and seeing the traces of strangers.

'You've come home at last.' Now she put both hands

on his cheeks and drew his head carefully towards her, as though she wanted to look closely at his face. He turned his head away, feeling her breath.

Later, when he was sitting at her table, she called him 'my Lukas'. She had to be well over eighty, her face was tiny and her mouth toothless, the teeth in a glass on the windowsill between potted cacti. 'I forget to water them, far too often, but it doesn't matter.'

She lived at the very top on the fourth floor and it had taken them a long time to get up there, him having to support her.

'You've come late,' she said, and again he didn't know what to answer.

He still hadn't said a word to her, but she had taken him by the hand and pulled him into her flat. She had made coffee and he had stood in the hall and waited and not known what to do, and had heard her hoarse voice from the kitchen. 'You really made your old grandma wait a long time.' Now they were sitting at the table, clutching their steaming cups, and the old woman's glasses fogged over. She slurped her coffee and he looked around. The furniture was old but definitely not antique. A large wall-unit with a glass cabinet containing glasses, china figurines and framed photos. A sofa with red cushions on it, a low table in front of it. Two armchairs. A clock ticking somewhere. Then he saw the grandfather clock in the corner by the door. Later, its gong chimed the hour. She clearly didn't forget to wind the clock up. 'All I had was the People's Solidarity carers,' the old woman said. 'I've missed you so much, my Lukas.'

'I don't know,' he said now, at last, 'how long I can stay...'

'No,' said the old woman, slamming her coffee cup down on the table so hard that the steaming coffee spilled over her hand, but she seemed not to feel it. 'No, you mustn't go back to that terrible country!'

'All right, all right,' he said to calm her down. She was gripping her cup the way she probably wanted to grab hold of him so he wouldn't go back to the terrible country, wherever it was. 'I'll be staying here for now, of course, I've only just got here.' And then he added, because she was still staring at him with big, upset, scared eyes through her glasses: 'Grandma.'

She nodded and slid her hand to the middle of the table, and he put his hand up to hers and briefly touched her fingertips, and she said: 'All I have is the People's Solidarity carers, I'm all alone apart from them.'

'When do they come, the People's Solidarity?' he asked. He knew the name, Volkssolidarität, it was some kind of association that took care of pensioners, he remembered a small, multi-storey building, that was where the People's Solidarity used to be, a sign with a written logo above the door. He hadn't known it still existed, it had been one of those East German things, but perhaps she just meant some kind of home-care service.

'I... I don't know exactly,' she said. 'They come quite often, the People's Solidarity people. I can hardly do my own shopping now, I can't always... and my medicine. After every letter, I thought, now... now my Lukas will soon be back.'

He felt himself getting tired, despite the coffee. It must be well after midnight. How often had the clock struck by now?

When the old woman left the room to fetch the letters Lukas had written to her, he realized his briefcase was missing. He could remember putting it down for a moment in the shop, downstairs. So it must still be down there. But what if someone saw it through the dusty

95

shop window? In the light of the day that would soon be breaking. Or had *they* perhaps even seen him running into the shop, as they chased him? No, then they would have followed him into the building.

Later, she told him it had been her shop, once. And he was surprised she was telling him, because her grandson Lukas must know that, but she'd told him a lot since he'd been back, because she'd 'been silent so long' while she waited for him. 'This is where my Lukas belongs.' A record shop, Record Chest, the ornate lettering even still legible above the dirty display window.

'I was so glad to get every letter,' she said as she put the pile of postcards and envelopes down on the table. He jumped. He must have nodded off.

'And at the same time, I was scared – you all alone in that terrible country.'

He was so tired and he wished they could sit on the armchairs or the sofa and not on the hard chairs at the dining table; the coffee was all gone. And then suddenly they were sitting on the armchairs, she had draped a blanket over him, even tucked it in over his shoulders so that only his head looked out over the blanket, but he hadn't felt any of it, and they had just been looking through the pile of letters and postcards he had sent her, from that terrible country.

'But I wasn't there on my own,' he said after he'd looked at some of the cards and letters, had read them. But the old woman was gone. Hadn't she just been sitting on the sofa? And telling him about her Record Chest, his letters on her lap...

And suddenly he heard music. Something classical; he didn't know much about classical music.

A piano tinkled, probably an old record, and then someone began to sing. What was the voice singing?

'*Fremd bin ich eingezogen...*' And then the old woman was back. She was standing behind him, he could tell, her hands on the broad back of the armchair, next to his shoulders. And while she sang along quietly in her hoarse voice, '*fremd zieh ich wieder aus,*' she sat down on the arm of the chair next to him and crossed her legs like a young woman, '*der Mai war mir gewogen mit manchem Blumenstrauß,*' and her stained grey nightshirt slipped up. '*Nun ist die Welt so trübe... der Weg gehüllt in Schnee.*'

It was only later that he saw the record player in her large bedroom. The room had two doors, one leading to the living room, the other to the hall. The flat was very large, five or six rooms in all, and Lukas had lived in one of them.

He lay on the bed, Lukas's bed, and looked at the letters again. How many he had sent: postcards, long letters with photos enclosed. He seemed to be about his age. Mid-thirties. Lukas at the mountains, Lukas by a river, Lukas in a Jeep, Lukas with locals, Lukas and the squaddies. 'Dear Grandma, I'm doing fine, even though I'm often homesick.'

It was quiet in the flat now. 'Put your old grandma to bed,' she had said once the last song had finished, nothing but crackling from the speakers, then the sound of the pickup arm clicking upwards and moving back, 'like I used to put you to bed, my Lukas.'

He had led her to her bedroom, but actually she had led him because he didn't know his way around this big unfamiliar flat, and she had leaned on him, her breathing heavy now, and once she'd lain down on the big bed he tucked her in, and she said, 'Stay a while, my Lukas, until I fall asleep.'

She sat up again, picked up the glass of water on the bedside table, and then he had to fetch some pills for her out of the bedside drawer, which was stuffed full of tablet boxes, and it took him some time to find the right ones, and she pushed the tablets between her lips with trembling hands and drank a sip of water. She coughed and swallowed and swallowed and had to wash it down with more water, and she drank until the glass was empty.

'Stay a while, my Lukas,' she said, 'until I fall asleep.'

'Of course,' he said, and he sat down on the edge of the bed and heard the ticking of the grandfather clock from the living room, saw the old woman's tiny face on the pillow, apparently shrunk with exhaustion, and she soon began to snore quietly. As he went to switch off the standing lamp, he saw a framed photo on the chest of drawers next to the bed, where the record player was as well. It was larger than the photos he'd looked at earlier in the living room. He had seen the old woman when she was young, in her Record Chest, a woman and a man, a wedding, a very long time ago, a Christmas tree, a girl in front of it, sitting on the floor, gifts. And in the bedroom, on the chest of drawers by the bed, he saw a child on the lap of his... grandmother. Lukas on his grandma's lap, a child with ruffled hair, perhaps three or four years. He remembered there had been a grandma-child in his class, back then. What had happened to his parents? Dead, didn't care (drinkers, possibly), gone away... Perhaps he and Lukas had been to the same cinema years ago, the Wintergarten or the Friendship Cinema, for the Sunday-morning children's film.

He looked at the old woman, who had stopped snoring and was lying perfectly still under the covers. In the photo, she was probably in her late fifties, and she looked old and young at the same time, in a strange way, she looked very strict while she held the boy with one hand.

For a moment he thought she was dead, lying there

like that under the covers, but then she started snoring quietly again, and he turned off the light and left the room.

'Dear Grandma, you can't imagine how people live here. Many of them are very poor. And most of them are really grateful we're here. The country is beautiful, I'm happy to be here, we're building it up, Grandma, but the war is coming from the mountains. I don't want to write that to you, but that's why we're here. Please don't worry, we're well protected and well equipped. I often think of you and I hope you're well and staying healthy. I'll be back soon.'

And he lay on the bed in Lukas's room, the letters by his side. He had undressed down to his underwear and crawled under the covers and listened to the flat and expected to hear footsteps on the stairs at any moment, Staff Sergeant Lukas, coming back from that 'beautiful country', as he called it, that 'terrible country' as the old woman had called it.

The next morning, he went shopping for her. When he'd woken up and found the old woman in the broad daylight pouring in through the living room windows, he had thought for a moment she would realize her mistake now, but she had just looked at him in brief confusion and then taken his hand and pressed it with her two small old hands and smiled and said quietly, 'Good morning, my Lukas,' as though he'd never been away.

Just as he opened the downstairs door on his way back – she had given him the keys and money – he heard voices in the stairwell. He ducked through the other door into the record shop, squatted on the floor and waited until he heard footsteps in the stairwell, coming down the stairs. The front door was opened and closed again and then all was quiet. He saw his briefcase against the wall.

A few rays of sunshine made it through the dirty window. He picked up the shopping bag and went back into the stairwell.

'What a shame,' said the old woman as he unpacked the shopping in the kitchen. 'You're a minute too late to meet the nice young lady from the People's Solidarity. She wanted to meet you, I've told her so much about you.'

'What did you tell her?' he asked as he put food in the fridge and on the table.

'I said my grandson's a hero, a real hero. An officer.'

'I'm only a sergeant, Grandma,' he said.

'Next time you'll be here when she comes. Then I can introduce you. She's a pretty young woman, my Lukas. Just the right age.'

'Grandma.'

They ate together in the living room. Grandma had cooked the gammon he'd bought at the butchers. Boiled potatoes to go with it. Weren't the windows open before? Dust in this light. Grandma had asked him to buy wine, so they drank wine with their meal.

'To your homecoming, my Lukas!'

A record was playing. Weren't they the same songs as the night before, as in the morning? *'Fremd bin ich eingezogen...'* Then the arm jumped up and a knocking, a hammering mixed into the crackling now coming out of the speakers, coming loud and steady from somewhere. At first, he was scared; was someone at the door? But then he realized: Grandma was making schnitzel. He heard her hammering the meat soft in the kitchen.

'I'm full up, Grandma,' he called. 'Thank you, Grandma.'

'My Lukas needs some proper food, not just kebabs!'

'They don't eat kebabs there, Grandma!'

But his grandma went on knocking and hammering.

'You can stop now, Grandma,' he called, 'it's softened up enough!'

'What do you say, my boy?'

'I'm sure the meat is soft enough now, Grandma!'

'I want it to melt in your mouth, my Lukas.' And his grandma went on and on hammering at the meat. 'It has to be like butter before the breadcrumbs go on.'

'It's all right, Grandma.'

When he closed his eyes, he felt the sun's rays on his face. When he closed his eyes and then blinked into the sunlight cast through the windows, he saw mountains, high mountains against a blue sky, he saw Jeeps, himself sitting in one of them, he saw a river reflecting the mountains and the sky, he saw fireworks in the night, he saw endless plains, he saw a young woman, the two of them walking arm in arm, him wearing a kind of dress uniform and she with her hand slipped under one of his epaulettes, he saw tents and barbed wire, he saw bearded men in long robes, he saw dark birds above the camp, above the river, he saw shapes in his grandma's stairwell, breaking in through the Record Chest, breaking in through the front door... 'Yugos, Turks,' he called out, so loud it echoed in the flat and the stairwell.

When he opened his eyes the living room was dark. All the doors and windows were wide open, but it seemed to be night again outside. 'Grandma?' he called out. He walked through the flat but he was alone. He lost his way in the rooms, none of the lights worked, he pressed the switches but the lamps wouldn't turn on, he confused the doors in the dusky light, then suddenly found his briefcase next to the table, and he opened it, an apple, his phone, his laptop, the phone battery dead, he opened his laptop, started it up and walked around the flat in the white light from the small screen, threw back the covers, dents in the pillows, he found a box room piled high with old records, their sleeves dusty, he looked out of one of the wide-open windows, the city dark too and the sky a strange grey.

Where had all the lights gone? But when he looked out of another of the large flat's windows he saw the brightly coloured streams of the street he had run down just yesterday. It almost seemed like the foreign cawing of the voices was reaching up to him from there. In the kitchen there was nothing but a piece of bloody meat on the table, the hammer-shaped mallet next to it. 'Grandma,' he called out. 'Where are you?'

How long had he slept? Light cast through the window. It must be daytime now. He was lying on the bed, between all the letters. He had thrown the covers on the floor in his sleep. He looked around the room. Shelves with model planes and models of tanks. A midi stereo system. A wardrobe. Later, he found the small crate with the uniform and the medals, under the bed. He had read the letters during the night. It had been an accident, apparently.

In the Jeep. That was what they wrote, at least.

He heard the old woman murmuring outside in the flat. He went and listened at the door. He heard her walking along the hall, stopping outside the door he was listening at, then continuing after a moment. He could hear how heavy her breathing was, almost wheezing.

Doors opening and closing, her footsteps elsewhere in the large flat, then she was back in the hall. He heard her hoarse whisper, '...told him not to go to that terrible... how can anyone be so stupid...' then she vanished into the other rooms, only to return shortly later. Sometimes not speaking and breathing heavily, then whispering uninterrupted in her hoarse voice, '...had it good here, how can anyone be so stupid, the poor boy, I'll give him what for when he gets back...' and he wondered where a woman well over eighty got so much strength.

He lay back down on the bed, between the letters. He knew she wouldn't come into the room.

He fell asleep again, then he woke up because he heard voices in the flat. It wasn't the old woman whispering outside the door; someone had come. He crept back to the door. A woman. A young voice. She seemed to be bringing food or cooking, he could smell it. Potatoes, and something that reminded him of school dinners. He heard her voice trying to calm the old woman down.

'Yes, of course he'll help you when he gets back. I wouldn't worry if I were you. You have to be patient, he'll be back soon. You know what young people are like...'

He tried to look through the keyhole but he couldn't make anything out in the hall; the draught hit him cold in the eye. 'I dream,' he heard the old woman very loud and very close, 'every night I dream of my boy. He's like my son, my Lukas, you see, he hasn't got anyone else, and I...' and again, the woman with the young voice said calming words. 'It's good that you dream of him, believe me, everything will be fine!' He heard footsteps and then it was quiet, and a little later the woman who had brought the food left the flat.

He waited one or two minutes, then he opened the window as quietly as he could and looked down. A blonde woman in a white coat came out of the house. She went to a van with Volkssolidarität printed on the side of it, parked by the pavement, and just before she got in she looked up at him. He jumped back, pressed himself to the wall, waited another one or two minutes and then closed the window.

He was hungry and thirsty. His briefcase was by the end of the bed, and he opened it and took out the apple that he took to work every day, and usually didn't eat until he got home, or the next day.

When evening came he put on the uniform. It was slightly too tight.

As he folded his trousers and put them on the bed, his keys fell out of the pocket. He remembered he had changed the locks at his flat at some point, and he put the keys on the bedside table.

He looked at the medals that had been in the box with the uniform. A silver cross on a black, red and yellow ribbon. On another black, red and yellow ribbon that held a kind of medallion with an eagle on it, large black letters spelled out the word for BATTLE. He put them in the pocket of his uniform jacket.

He sat on the edge of the bed until night fell again. He heard the old woman moving around the flat, music again and the crackle of the record, and then quiet again.

He cautiously opened the door of his room and walked into the hall. He suddenly felt an urgent need to pee, and he tried to remember where the bathroom was.

He saw that the door to the old woman's bedroom was ajar as he went to the bathroom. The floorboards creaked, and it seemed as if the creaking got louder and louder the more carefully he crept along the hall. And when he had almost reached the bathroom door, the creaks of the old wood became groans, as though the boards were sighing beneath his feet, and he stopped a few times so that the creaking and groaning would fall silent at last, stopped and listened, but he heard nothing behind the bedroom door; she seemed to be asleep. Only the grandfather clock in the living room ticking.

He stood by the basin and retched. Just before, he had lifted the toilet lid for a second and instantly let go again, and it clanged against the porcelain.

He washed his face, it looked very pale in the mirror, above his green uniform jacket. Why did nobody clean the damn toilet? What did the People's Solidarity come for? He washed his face. A long grey hair adhered between his fingers. He tried to wipe it off on the edge of the basin, but he couldn't get rid of it and he held his hand underneath the running tap.

He laid his hand against the mirror's glass, saw the flat hands slowly touching, then he used the other hand to turn off the light, with the switch next to the mirror. He stood in the bathroom a while longer, then he went into the hall and along the hall into her bedroom.

He heard her snoring as he went up to her bed. He sat down on the chair next to the bedside table.

Her mouth was open, her lips collapsed, almost disappearing into the dark opening of her snoring mouth. The glass of water containing her teeth was on the bedside table. The drawer was open and he saw the white plastic strips of tablets. 'Grandma,' he whispered, touching her face. He leaned forwards and felt his arm muscles hardening under the sleeves of the uniform jacket. Had she opened her eyes for a moment and then smiled when she saw him? He had taken the toilet brush and cleaned the bowl after he'd stood in front of the mirror in the bathroom, had run the brush around the porcelain oval over and over, had pressed the brush firmly into the water at the opening, poured cleaning fluid into the bowl, had cleaned, walked through all the rooms in the flat. Closed all the doors. Grandma was lying under the covers, only her forehead and her hair visible. So white.

He heard his footsteps in the stairwell. Before he

opened the front door, he stroked his uniform smooth, felt the medals in the side pocket of his uniform jacket and pinned them to the fabric, although he didn't know exactly where he ought to pin them. Then he opened the door and stepped outside the building. It was night again, still night, and he set off, towards the bridge, towards the big birds, towards the street along which he had once come.

DARK SATELLITES

It's all a while ago now. And just because it's coming up again and I'm remembering those long nights, because it was summer at the time, and I'm remembering those long bright days and that one night, it's got nothing to do with the whole religious and political thing, whatever you call it, being suddenly present again. What's the present, anyway? Nothing. We're in a whole different place now. And I know what I'm talking about, I know all about presence in the moment, because I run a burger bar, in a single-storey building with a roof projecting over it, which used to be a petrol station.

Back then I lived in one of the high-rises next to the municipal park, up on the fourteenth floor, and when I looked out of the window in the stairwell, where I'd sometimes have a smoke in the evening and look out over the town, I could spot my little burger bar even though it was more than two kilometres away. I'd paint-ed the outside of the petrol station red, it had been my business partner Mario's idea when we opened up the burger bar together.

'Who's Mario, tell me about Mario.'

'Mario is an old friend, we met in the navy.'

'When were you in the navy?'

'Few years ago now. We were cooks, on a ship.'

'On a ship?'

'Yeah, on a ship. Up on the coast. And Mario was an even worse cook than me.'

'I don't believe a word of it.'

'It's the truth, we cooked all sorts of crap in that kitch-en, it was crazy.'

'But you've got a chef's hands. And your Hamburger Special and your potato salad...'

'Yeah, they're good. You're right there, they're really good. And the potato salad recipe is from my grandma.'

'And your old friend Mario, where is he now?'

'Went back up to the coast, had this idea about a floating burger bar...'

'A floating burger bar?'

'Yeah. Some kind of tourist thing. He always had crazy ideas, Mario did.'

We were standing by the window in the stairwell and smoking and looking down at the town.

We met almost every evening by the window in the stairwell – she was a secret smoker.

She lived on the same floor as me, with Hamed, her boyfriend.

Hamed sometimes came to my burger bar for lunch and got a steak sandwich and drank a Coke or a tea. He worked in a huge internet café a few roads along, where the Arabs had their neighbourhood. Neighbourhood's a bit of an exaggeration, to be honest. It was actually just a very wide, very long street all the way to the eastern edge of town, and on both sides, there were rows and rows of kebab shops and phone shops and second-hand shops and junk shops, and there were loads of internet cafés as well. And somewhere along there was the internet café where Hamed worked. I never visited him there, it wasn't a part of town where I felt all that comfortable. The big internet café belonged to a cousin of Hamed's, apparently, but I didn't really care. For a long time, I didn't know exactly where Hamed was from. Kuwait? Iraq? Or was it Lebanon? But that wasn't all that important either, even though Mario and I had often used to sit at the map table on our ship and look at all the countries and the seas and drink out of his hip flask with the engraved KGB emblem, which he'd bought off an old Russian officer, at the end of the nineties, that was, and the old man, our Captain, who was actually only the head of the ship's galley, he'd sometimes tell us about the first Gulf War when he was in the Mediterranean, 'cruising off the coasts of the Orient', as he put it. It's all long ago now, the first war and the second one and all that. But I said that already.

The first time Hamed came to my burger bar was just before closing time, and I was inspecting the carpet as usual. The carpet covered the floor from the counter to the door, and it reminded me every day of my old friend Mario because it had been his idea to lay carpet in my burger bar, which had been *our* burger bar to begin with. 'It'll make it feel cosy,' he'd said. 'People will feel good straight away, they'll feel at home, or even better, like on a red carpet! And it goes nicely with the paint.'

But carpet in a burger bar is nothing but trouble. There were two plastic tables in front of the counter, and when people ate their hamburgers or sausages there, they'd always spill ketchup, mayonnaise or mustard on the floor, or on the carpet, actually.

And in the winter people would trail mushy snow and mud into my burger bar, and although dog-owners were gradually starting to pack up their dogs' dirt in little plastic bags and then throw them in the bin, there were still plenty of dog turds on the streets, and all that dirt, with snow or without snow, with mud or without mud, would be stuck to people's shoes, and the dark-red carpet got dirtier and dirtier, darker and darker.

I had replaced it a couple of times and a company came at the end of each month with a carpet-cleaning machine, and it was probably only because it reminded me of my old friend Mario that I kept the stupid carpet for so long.

'Tiles are better,' Hamed said, and I got a fright. I'd been stabbing away with a burger flipper at the carpet, which had got hard spots again. I turned around and tried to hide the burger flipper behind my back, but he seemed not to see it and he said again, 'Tiles are better.'

I slotted the burger flipper into my belt behind my back, turned to face the late customer and the two of us looked down at the carpet. 'Yes,' I said, 'tiles would be better.'

It was only then I realized I knew him from the high-rise, had seen him a few times before in the corridor or the lift, and I asked, 'Fourteenth floor?' and he nodded and said, 'Fourteenth floor,' and then he introduced himself, and I introduced myself, and we shook hands.

'I see you sometimes,' he said, 'early, very early... you come here.'

'Yes,' I said, 'very early. Almost still night.'

'For a while,' he said, 'I have work on a building site. So I leave the house very early too.'

'In the summer,' I said, 'I like to walk. Leave the car here. It's a nice walk across town.'

'Your burger bar is good, very good.' He looked around and gave an approving nod. 'I think, we are neighbours and I...'

'Well, almost,' I said.

'Neighbours,' he said again. It wasn't until later that I realized *being neighbours* was an important thing for him, it was a tradition, an old custom, to pay visits and that kind of thing, back where he came from. 'And I see you go in here, every morning...'

'Every morning.' I tapped my forefinger three times against the counter, probably to make sure everything stayed that way, me getting up early and my burger bar and so on.

'And then I think...'

'You'd come by. Do you want something to eat, or a coffee? On the house.'

At first, I wanted to offer him a beer, but then I'd seen his prayer beads, held between forefinger and thumb of his right hand. He moved the beads very slowly between his fingers while he spoke.

'You have tea?'

'Sure,' I said, 'Earl Grey.'

I put the 'closed' sign on the door, it was just after eight, and we drank a cup of tea together. I had to go back to the storeroom first to get a new pack of tea bags. Most people who ate in my place drank coffee or beer or Coke and I wasn't much of a tea-drinker either. Hamed wanted to know how I ran my burger bar, where I got my meat and my salad from, and if I had anything without pork in it.

'Sure I do,' I said. 'I've got loads of beef here. OK; the Hamburger Specials are half and half.'

'Half and half?'

'Minced beef and pork, mixed.'

'We Muslims,' he said, 'you know...'

'Yeah, yeah,' I said, 'I know. No problem. I've got... no, wait, the original Thüringens, there's pork in them, of course.'

'Thüringens,' he said, 'those are the famous sausages?'

'Do they know them back there as well? I mean, where you're from?'

And then I told him what's in Thüringen sausages and how they're made and how I grill them really nicely over charcoal.

'And you have nothing without pork?'

'No, I do,' I said, 'steaks, good beef steaks.' We were standing in front of the counter on Mario's grubby carpet, drinking our tea. I pointed to the big board listing all the dishes, above the till. 'Look, my famous Nine-Eleven Steak Sandwich.'

'Nine-eleven steak sandwich?' He looked at me, leaned his head to one side, and took off his glasses. He was smooth-shaven, wore round glasses and didn't look like one of those mullahs you heard so much about, even then. He looked over at the board of dishes and prices, put his glasses on and off again, then he looked at me and smiled.

'Just kidding,' I said. 'New York Steak Sandwich, see?' I pointed at the board. I charged three ninety for it. I hated ninety-nine-cent prices.

Fifty-cent prices were my favourite, like three fifty for example, or round numbers like one mark, euro now of course, but I often remembered a sausage stall in my childhood, it was next door to a cinema, one mark for a sausage. You had to move with the times, though, and three fifty didn't make me enough profit, but my one-euro coffee was a classic. There were still plenty of building sites, always will be, and the builders came every morning and every lunchtime.

'Nine-eleven steak sandwich.' He was still smiling, and shaking his head.

'You have to try my famous nine... New York steak sandwich.' I went behind the counter to the grill. I had a pretty fresh steak on a piece of silver foil that was going to be my dinner. I had a charcoal grill and an electric grill. My burger bar was really tiny – I noticed it again as I was making Hamed his famous steak sandwich. It had been a very small petrol station, from the days when sausages only cost a mark off the grill. My steak sandwich for three fifty wasn't really famous – most people came for my Hamburger Special or the potato salad.

Hamed leaned over the counter. 'Forgive me, sir,' he said, 'but...'

'No need to stand on formalities,' I said. 'And what's to forgive?'

I was chopping tomato and cucumber because they were part of my steak sandwich, even though the really famous steak sandwich in New York worked without cucumber and tomato. My old friend Mario had told me about steak sandwiches. He'd been in New York for a while at the end of the nineties, or at least he always said he had.

'I only want to ask,' he said, uncertainly eyeing the grill and the worktop where I was thinly slicing the tomato and cucumber, 'if the pork meat and the steak... they must not touch.'

'No,' I said, pointing the knife at the grill. 'Everything has its place. The hamburgers go there and the sausages go there... and I usually do the steaks here on the electric grill.' That wasn't actually true, I only used the electric grill if I was running out of charcoal or if I had to make up a few orders in advance, but what did it matter if the steak for my steak sandwich got a bit of pork fat on it...?

'No, no, you mustn't see it like that. Hamed's very precise, we're very precise about it. We want to be pure.'

'And you reckon God doesn't like my sausages?' We were standing by the window and smoking. As usual, I had opened the little window in the stairwell with the Allen key I kept on my keyring. The windows were all locked so no one could jump out, and there were smoke alarms everywhere, except on the stairwell. It was made of concrete, the walls, the steps, and it was almost always empty and quiet because we had the two lifts, but in the evenings came the smokers who weren't allowed to smoke in their flats any more, because their wives or husbands wouldn't let them or because they had kids. The clicking of the lighters, the banging of the doors, the coughs, quiet conversations sometimes floated through the neon-lit stairwell in the evenings, like the smoke from the cigarettes.

For a while, I'd run all the way up the fifteen floors when I got home from the burger bar after work, because I thought I ought to do something to keep fit, I stood still all day, and because my back doctor said climbing stairs was good, it'd keep my vertebrae nice and flexible.

She smoked, and she pushed her headscarf back a bit, and a few locks of hair fell onto her forehead. She closed her eyes, blew out the smoke and held her head into the wind, tipped her head back and the wind moved the strands of her hair. We stood by the open window while night came slowly outside, but it was still light, the sky turned pink and red, and then it seemed like it was getting lighter again, just before night fell, pale pink, pale red, and we were surprised how long the daylight lingered, those nights.

She pushed her headscarf back over her forehead, ran both hands over it, and for a moment it looked like she was covering her cheeks with the fabric.

She had acne scars, they were very obvious because her skin was almost white, like chalk, you might say, like white chicken meat, *I'd* say, and she tugged her headscarf over the little red lines and scars on her pale cheeks. She was a few years younger than Hamed, in her early twenties, twenty-five at most, and very tall and very thin.

'Allah is great, Allah is merciful,' she said, and she leaned forward and put out her cigarette in the little ash-tray I'd shaped out of silver foil – I always had a roll of silver foil with me when we met in the stairwell – and I put my finished cigarette next to hers and scrunched

114

the ashtray up into a silver ball, about to throw it out the window. She grabbed my arm.

'Don't! Imagine if you hit someone.'

'But there's the roof down there, over the entrance.'

She shook her head and pulled my arm with the scrunched-up ashtray away from the window. 'What if a gust of wind comes? It could get blown anywhere...'

'It's just a ball of silver foil,' I said, and shoved it in the side pocket of my hoodie, and her hand slid down my arm. The hoodie was red, dark red like my burger bar, with the name of my burger bar printed on it. I put the hood up and said, 'Now I'm covering my head, to make God happy.'

'Why are you saying that? God is merciful, God is great.' She looked at me, very serious. She really seemed to be angry. I often made jokes like that when we smoked together in the stairwell. After work, Hamed and his friends went to Little Arabia, that was what we called the neighbourhood where the internet café was, where he worked, but she couldn't even smoke in the flat when Hamed wasn't in. A few of Hamed's friends smoked when they came to visit our high-rise, mind you, but that was different.

'Yes,' I said, 'he probably is very merciful. And he doesn't mind you smoking.' I held out my pack to her again. She took one out and I lit myself a new one as well. I'd make a new ashtray out of silver foil in a minute. We sat down on the top step and our footsteps echoed in the stairwell, sounds a few floors down like someone was answering to our footsteps, doors closing, night smokers who didn't want to go down and outside, even though it was still light, those long short nights.

'The Quran doesn't say anything about cigarettes,' she said, and nodded and smoked and held her cigarette so tightly between forefinger and thumb that the filter was squashed a few minutes later, when she put the smoked cigarette in the new silver-foil ashtray I had put on the concrete floor between us, where my cigarette was smoking too, the embers almost down to the filter. I screwed up the silver ashtray again before she could extinguish the cigarette not mentioned in the Quran, and a very small and very thin line of smoke rose from the silvery skin of the silvery ball. I shoved the screwed-up ashtray in with the other one in the side pocket of my hoodie. I felt the crumpled silver foil warm on my hand and pressed it harder. She stood up, and I stood up as well.

'I've got an early start in the morning,' I said. 'Say hi to Hamed from me.' We were standing with our backs to the door leading to our floor, looking down at the steps leading to the lower floors. Later that night I went for a walk in the municipal park and drank a beer because I couldn't sleep, and counted the storeys of our high-rise and tried to find the window we'd been standing by, earlier on.

'I... I'll be off, then. Say hi to Hamed from me.' Hadn't I just said that?

I wanted to give her my hand, it was half-raised already, but then I didn't.

The first time I went for a cup of tea in Hamed's flat, I held out my hand for her to shake but she took a step back, lowered her head slightly and said, 'Sorry, but Allah doesn't want...'

'Sorry,' I said. 'I forgot Allah doesn't...' Wasn't her hand on my arm, earlier on? I stepped back, behind me the door leading out of the stairwell to the fifteenth floor. Then I went back towards her and raised my hand to chest height and then a bit higher, and my palm almost touched her face before I put my arm down again.

'Don't,' she said, and her face blushed, and her acne scars were plain to see now too, almost glowing on her face. Her headscarf had slipped low over her forehead.

'Don't,' she said again. She lived with Hamed on my floor, just a few flats down. She came from here, from our town, and until she met Hamed she hadn't believed in anything and had shook hands with anyone. I don't know exactly where they met and how. Actually, I used to know it, Hamed told me once, but why should I think about their story much? My old friend Mario, who had gone back up to the coast to open some floating burger bar there, would have said, 'What do you want from *her*?'

And I would have said, 'Nothing, Mario, what gave you that idea?'

And the first time Hamed came to my burger bar and I made him the nine-eleven steak sandwich, I'd never imagined that not long after I would be visiting him at his mosque that was somewhere in our town, a place I'd never seen, I hadn't even known there was a mosque in our town, and then when I was there because I wanted to see *her* in the mosque, because she went to mosque with Hamed, every Friday and sometimes during the week... but I'm getting my times muddled up, because weeks and months did pass, and I drank tea with Hamed in Hamed's flat and smoked secretly with his girlfriend in the stairwell, by the window, before I even set foot in the mosque, but I already said that the present is nothing.

'You can see the lights of the satellites at this time.'

'You mustn't touch me, I mustn't touch you. Allah...'

'I know, I know, I just want to...'

'What satellites and what lights do you mean? The moon?'

She had sat down on the stairs.

'That too,' I said, 'but I mean the buildings, the... it'll be a few minutes more. When it's properly dark.'

'I have to get back to Hamed,' she said and turned her head to me, propped on both her hands, covering her cheeks and her acne scars. 'Hamed will be home soon.'

'Stay a few more minutes,' I said again and sat down next to her. 'It's light for a long time in summer.'

'Are the nights longer or shorter now?' she asked, looking at me.

'I don't know.' I shoved my hands in the side pockets of my hoodie.

No warm silver balls. I had brought a glass ashtray with me, now on the step in front of us.

'I don't know,' I said. 'For me, night starts when I finish work, so at eight. Whether it's light or dark.'

'So the nights are...' she hesitated. 'They're always the same?'

'No, they're not,' I said, and I put my hand on her shoulder, close to her neck, at that place where a slight slope rises, a narrow hill, a muscle or something leading to the neck, a slight narrow slope, I don't know what to call it.

Later, in the municipal park where I went for a walk almost every night at that point, once it had finally got dark, I counted the floors of our high-rise, thought of her pointy shoulder bones, and in the morning, when I put a piece of shoulder on the grill in my burger bar, beef, pork, what does it matter, I ran my hand along the still half-frozen meat, there it was, that shoulder bone... stroked her cool shoulder, the charcoal steam rising to my eyes, I was tired and I could have used my old friend Mario, who was going bust somewhere on the coast with his floating burger bar, probably. I thought of Hamed,

118

her boyfriend, who she usually called 'my husband'.

'I have to go home, home to my husband.'

'Where are you from?'

'What do you mean, where am I... How do you mean?' She looked at me, her headscarf pulled over both cheeks like she was ashamed of the acne scars that ploughed red lines across her face.

'I mean... who... where are you from? Here in town? Or somewhere else.'

And she was sitting back next to me on the stairs, come back from the door she'd just been about to walk through.

'Hamed was very good to me. My husband's very good to me.'

I nodded. 'Hamed's a good guy.'

She told me about her family, where she was from, here in our town.

'Hamed likes you a lot,' she said then, and rested her head on her palms again and hid her red scars as she sat on the stairs. And I was still holding the pack of cigarettes in my hand when I got to my flat – 'Want another one?' – I'd been holding it so long the thin transparent foil around the box was clammy and warm, and the palm of my hand was damp too, and I threw the box on the sofa, where it nestled among the last few days' and weeks' newspapers, which I read there every morning before I went to my burger bar. I always read a day behind, I brought the papers home in the evening and chucked them on the sofa and then read them in the morning. I almost always woke up before my alarm. But it was only my phone, the alarm-clock function ringing. My favourite old alarm clock, an ancient mechanical bugger my grandma had given me many years ago, was up on the coast now with my old friend Mario, where he was trying out some kind of floating burger bar or chip shop. He'd always really liked my alarm clock, that old thing had got us out of our bunks before alarm-clock functions on phones did the job, and I'd given him the huge old bugger when he went back up to the coast where we'd fed the whole of the navy.

Sometimes you lose yourself in time, you know, and it takes a few seconds to work out where you are. It was probably summer. I was smoking and looking down at the dark satellite towns, hardly visible by then because the last lights in the windows were going out, far behind the municipal park.

'When the sky is rent as thunder; when the stars scatter and the oceans merge together...'

'OK, OK,' I said, 'and what is that supposed to tell me?'

'That the Lord is here for us,' Hamed said, 'that he'll redeem us. It goes on...'

'What, more?' I asked. 'After the redemption?' I flipped two steaks and turned back to Hamed, who was leaning on the counter, drinking a cup of Earl Grey. Two builders were at the tall table outside, smoking and drinking the beers I'd sold them a few minutes earlier. It was their steaks I was grilling. The end of the working day, and it was growing slowly dark again. Was it still summer, and the days were meeting the nights?

'No,' said Hamed, 'the sura, you see? The sura goes on, the sura about the... how do you say... rent as thunder, when the sky breaks...'

'Rent asunder,' I said. 'You mean *asunder*, not *as thunder*. When the sky is rent asunder. Sura number eighty-something.'

'How you... how do you know about the sura?'

'Oh yeah, that surprised you, didn't it?' I turned

around to take care of a Thüringen sausage I had on the charcoal grill for one of the guys who'd gone outside for a smoke before I could get the cash off him, and then he'd just left, even though my sausages looked good, my Thüringen sausages were almost legendary, in our neighbourhood, in our town. 'Your new Middle Eastern friend is no good for business,' my old friend Mario would have said. I missed him a lot at that time, and he was probably right, but then again, he'd dragged in all sorts of characters himself when we were running the burger bar together, before he went back up to the coast to open a floating burger bar or chip shop or whatever it was. Mario had a few friends in and around Little Arabia who sold drugs. My old friend Mario was partial to the stuff his friends used to deal, now and then, but it had never been a problem.

'They are not men,' said Hamed, 'with no God. Not good men, you deny the Judgement.'

'You keep out of it, Ay-rab,' said my old friend Mario, 'you concentrate on your brainwashed girlfriend...'

'Shut it, Mario,' I said.

I put the steaks on two paper plates for the builders waiting and smoking outside, end of the working day, cut open bread rolls, put grilled onions on top of the steaks, cut open bread rolls, stirred the pot of my special steak mustard, flipped the steaks, it was nearly the end of my working day too and the charcoal was well done, not much more than a low pile of embers, hardly visible under the grey and white hood of ash, heating and grilling the meat I'd got from the cash-and-carry that morning.

'O man, who labour constantly to meet your Lord, shall you meet him,' I said, and I put the two steak rolls, not to be confused with my famous steak sandwich, on two paper plates. Hamed thought for a moment and nodded, put his paper cup of Earl Grey on the counter and looked at me and moved his prayer beads between forefinger and thumb.

'He shall have a lenient reckoning,' I said, trying to remember the exact wording, and handed the two paper plates to the two builders, who had been watching me hungrily through the glass and had come inside.

'And he shall go back rejoicing to his people,' I said, and the two of them looked around again, raised their hands to say goodbye, regulars, and I said goodbye as well, and I saw them talking outside, whispering, their heads drawn in close as though I could hear them through the window of my burger bar, and they turned back briefly to look at me. They laughed – did they grin? – before they turned down a side street.

'And he shall burn in the fire of Hell,' said Hamed while I was cleaning the grill and clearing the worktop. And I joined in: 'I swear by the glow of sunset; by the night, and all that it brings together; by the moon, in her full perfection...'

Should I tell him I'd bought it, the book, in a shop in our town centre, because she, because his wife... Should I tell him I read it because I wanted to understand *her*?

'Where are you from?'

And she told me her story.

And Hamed smiled, hugged me as I untied my apron and came over to him at the plastic table where he'd put down his prayer beads. 'It is time,' he said, 'it is time to pray. You have...?'

'A rug?' I asked.

'Yes, something like this.' Hamed was already kneeling on the tiles. The weekend before, I had torn up the red carpet my old friend Mario had talked me into and got the whole place tiled. Hamed had got hold of a man for me, an Arab or something, who did it cash-in-hand. But now Hamed wanted to pray and my tiles were too hard, and his God loved rugs.

'A rug... Hold on a mo.' I went back to my junk room and I did find a piece of the red roll I'd used to carpet my burger bar. If Mario knew the remains of the red carpet he'd been so into would be used as a prayer mat by an Arab... 'Dining on red carpet, it's great advertising, you get it, eating like movie stars!'

'Let's open a burger bar, Mario.'

'Sure, let's. The red-carpet burger bar. Red, get it? Eye ketchup!'

'What about ketchup, Mario?'

'Like eye catcher, get it? Cause it's red. Our burger bar!'

'Yeah, a burger bar, Mario.'

'Eye catcher!'

And Hamed kneeled down on the scrap of red carpet I'd cut off the roll with a sharp steak knife. And he prayed there on the new tiled floor of my little burger bar, murmured the unfamiliar words and phrases of his unfamiliar language. A couple of passers-by stopped and looked through the big glass window, and I crept past Hamed and put the Closed sign on the door.

Bowing down... she knew all those religious verses off by heart, partly in Hamed's language, partly in ours, and she bowed down. I stood next to her and she bowed down, kneeling in the corridor of our high-rise, her head facing Mecca or the place where she thought it was, and her T-shirt rose upwards, she always wore very loose T-shirts and very loose trousers or skirts, even though she was so thin and bony, her loose T-shirt rose up as she pressed her upper body to the floor of the high-rise, and I wanted to kneel down next to her, lie down next to her, kneel down behind her, yes, that too.

'What do you want from *her*?' my old friend Mario would have asked.

'I don't know,' I'd have said, 'that's just the way it is sometimes, Mario.' And Mario nodded and patted me on the shoulder. 'That's just the way it is sometimes.'

I'd never had much time for religion and all that. My grandma, the one who gave me the alarm clock and the recipe for potato salad, used to take me to church on Christmas Eve when I was little, but that was about it. And the nights, the evenings when I was reading the book, the one I'd bought because of her, it was like far-away worlds, like Sinbad the Sailor or Ali Baba and the Forty Thieves – ('Sinbad, Ali Baba? They're kid's stories!'

'Shut it, Mario, or come back and help me with the burger bar.'

'With *her*, you mean.'

'No, I'd never ask you for help with that.'

'I never got it, the whole religious crap. It's like the Lord of the Rings for me.'

'That's what I said, Sinbad, Ali Baba.') – fairy-tales I'd once read as a child or knew from the cinema or TV.

'No,' she said, 'you mustn't see it like that, we want to be pure before God... He speaks to us, every day.'

'Don't get me wrong, I think it's good, but...'

'Hamed wants you to come with him. To our mosque.'

'Do you think it's allowed? I wouldn't mind. You'll come too, won't you?'

'Of course.'

'All right... But I have to be honest, I...'

'That doesn't matter.' She looked at me and shook her head and nodded. She had something defiant and lenient about her at the same time, and her acne scars glowed red on her pale face. We were sitting on the stairs, smoking. The window was wide open and it was getting dark outside, and the wind whistled through the stairwell. Was it still late summer or was it autumn already? Later, when it snowed and I stayed in my burger bar and worked until late into the night – I'd extended my opening hours and added mulled wine to the menu on the board – I often thought about it. Had I shown her the dark satellites? Those tall high-rises on the edge of town where the lights went out slowly in the night, flat by flat, window by window, and I saw us standing by the window and I counted the floors when I came home and smoked my after-work cigarette downstairs, outside the building, even though it was cold and I had to stamp my cold feet against the snow.

'Which way is east?'

'I don't know exactly. Over there?'

'I have to pray facing east...'

'I know.' I touched her face. Gently stroked my fingers over the acne scars that ploughed red lines across her face.

Hamed had asked the same thing: 'Which way is east?' before he knelt down on the scrap of red I'd put on the tiles in front of him.

'I don't know exactly... Over there.'

And then, as they prayed, I realized they were actually praying towards the north, or more like northwest, because the big road my burger bar was on led north out of the town, and the corridor in our high-rise where we used to meet pointed northwest, more west than the road, and behind the municipal park that gave me my bearings were the satellites, that was where the new estate rose to the sky, the high towers on the edge of the town, behind which the sun went down. The land of the

125

setting sun.

I stroked her face and she was perfectly silent, and then she leaned her head on my shoulder. I took her in my arms and held her tight, and our cigarettes smoked in the glass ashtray on the step in front of us, which had been replacing the silver paper for a while by then, until the orange touched the filter and burned out.

I wanted to see her hair, run my fingers through her hair, she had short, red-blonde hair that only peeked out at the sides of her headscarf, sometimes a few locks on her forehead.

My hand was on her headscarf and she said, 'No, don't,' and she pushed my hand away, and I hugged her again, held her tight, and she let it happen, pressed herself against me, lay heavy on and by me, even though she was so thin and bony.

Later too, much later, not that evening and not the next one, when she lay naked next to me, lay on my bed, her hair was still under her headscarf.

'We used to wear a head covering to cook as well, remember?'

'That's totally different, Mario.'

'Well, just think about it.'

'Think about what?'

'About all this headscarf crap. I mean, it's unhygienic to cook with your hair uncovered. Who wants a hair on their steak? But what does God care...'

'Since when have you believed in God, Mario?'

'Exactly. And how about sex? Bare-headed or not?'

I looked through the gap in the door, left ajar, into the women's mosque, headscarves lined up in rows, now they were kneeling and bowing down, and her red-blonde underneath one of the headscarves.

I tried to spot her in the crowd of praying women.

126

She'd vanished into the flat next door to the men's mosque only a few minutes ago, she'd turned back to me and Hamed and smiled. Her smile, the gentle red of her acne scars that were so visible when she... The flats they called the *mosque* were on the third floor of a dilapidated residential building, west of the satellites we saw in the nights. I hadn't known women and men prayed in separate flats. And after the big prayer, when they feasted, invited their guest to eat with them, when I sat on the floor with them and ate with them from the big plastic sheet, she didn't show up. I went out to the stairs again to see her. Saw the women and children through the gap in the door, left ajar, the praying over there too and the food being made. Where was she? Someone touched my shoulder. Hamed was standing behind me. 'Come back and eat, my friend. You are our guest today. God sees us, and God loves us.' He put his arm around me and we went back into the men's section of the mosque. I understood the separation, the division, I thought about it while I sat on the floor with the Arabs and ate rice and meat that tasted like mutton and had been stewed a tad too little, and drank strong, sweet tea. If she'd been sitting somewhere in front of me or next to me, during the prayers, during the meal, but especially during the prayers, I mean if I'd been a believer, I wouldn't have had eyes or ears for God. While they prayed and their preacher, the imam I mean, spoke and I didn't understand a word, I had leaned against the wall at the back, lowered my head when they bowed down, lowered my head to my chest to show my respect, never mind the Lord of the Rings. I had brought my book, I'd bought it a few weeks earlier because I wanted to understand what she believed in; I had it resting on my lap, and while the Arabs prayed I saw that the pages were covered in

127

grease stains, the murmuring and the incomprehensible voices around me, in front of me, I had read the book on my worktop, with greasy fingers, while the meat sizzled on the grill. Then I'd gone on reading at home, and then I'd read it in the stairwell while I waited for her, and when I heard footsteps in the hall – her footsteps? – I stuck the book in the waistband of my jeans, under my hoodie. 'Darkness upon darkness. If he stretches out his hand he can scarcely see it. Indeed the man from whom God withholds His light shall find no light at all...'

Had I shown her the dark satellites behind the municipal park? Their lights went out, window by window, flat by flat, as the night set in, until only the outlines of the tall buildings were visible, far behind the municipal park.

'God is angry,' she said, 'God hates me.' She was standing outside my front door and I could instantly tell she was drunk. Her headscarf had slipped out of place and her red-blonde hair was falling down over her face. I'd never seen her hair like that, and if she hadn't been drunk, I'd have brushed the red-blonde locks carefully aside. Her face was very white, as pale as chalk, you might say, as white as chicken meat, *I'd* say, and her acne scars stood out more than usual. 'God is angry,' she said, 'He hates me.'

'Don't talk crap,' I said, and as I took a step towards her to bring her inside, she stumbled against me. She smelled strongly of cigarettes and pubs and drink.

I pushed the door closed with my foot and led her along the hall into my living room.

She tried to tear herself away, and she started to cry and she wanted to bang her head against the wall, but I held her by the shoulders and pulled her to the sofa.

'Everything's fine,' I said. 'Shhh, shhh. Everything's

fine,' and I stroked her shoulder and her neck, which was covered by the triangle of her headscarf.

She had been back to where she came from. Where she'd still be if she hadn't met Hamed. I adjusted her headscarf, brushed her hair out of her face, tried to lay her down on the sofa, but she wanted to get up again, hugging me and speaking quietly against my chest, against my upper body. 'It's fine,' I said, 'everything's going to be fine, you just have to sleep. Just go to sleep now.'

I felt my T-shirt getting wet. She rolled off the sofa, I tried to hold her back and then she was lying on the floor, and I lay down with her.

I pressed her against me. I took off her clothes; they stank and they were wet. The rugs on the walls of the mosque, women's section, men's section, the mosque that was actually two flats, in a dilapidated building. The gap in the door that I looked through, at the rugs with the illegible letters, at the praying women's headscarves. And when I looked for her there, her red-blonde hair that I ran my fingers through, carefully so as not to wake her.

I had put her in my bed. She had been back to where she came from. Where she'd still be...

I stood outside our high-rise and counted the floors and tried to find our window and stamped my feet against the snow.

I worked longer hours now, I sold mulled wine, the builders came and went, and my home-made mulled wine was a hit. The tiles were great and I wished my old friend Mario was working with me on the tiles that Hamed had got me.

I sometimes had crazy dreams, and in my dreams I was lost in the corridors of our high-rise, and I came to the flat where she lived with Hamed. The door was open, left ajar, and I went in. We had sometimes drunk tea there, Hamed next to me, and she'd sit on a chair behind us, against the wall. How often I turned around to her. She smiled and raised her hand and pretended she was holding a cigarette between forefinger and thumb, and moved it slowly to her mouth.

But the flat was empty. And I was lost in there, and I was looking for her. Their bedroom looked like my bedroom. And then I saw that all the windows were open. And fear gripped me in my dream. And I ran to one of the open windows and leaned out.

And in those crazy dreams I'm so scared I'll see her down there when I look out. My dark-red burger bar is far behind the buildings and doesn't come into it. And I lean out of the window, so scared I'll see her down there. Her body on the projecting roof above the entrance, her body in the snow. Someone bangs on the door. And then I wake up.

'I have to go home, I have to go to Hamed.'

'Stay a bit longer. The satellites.'

'What do you mean? The moon?'

'That too. Sometimes the moon's above them.'

'Do we have to wait until it gets dark?'

'It's almost dark now.'

'Hold me.'

'Yes.'

No, no one had knocked at my door. I went to their flat, which was on the same floor, we were almost neighbours, and rang the doorbell, and later all I did was knock gently because I didn't want to hear the loud *ding-dong* of the bell seeming to echo in the corridor, but they didn't open the door, not Hamed, not her. Winter came, spring came, I worked long hours and came home very late, and at some point they were gone, moved out, left

130

the high-rise, and I stood downstairs in the slush and snow and counted the floors.

I had brought her back to Hamed the morning after that night when she'd been standing outside my front door drunk, when she lay naked in my bed, and I nearly went crazy because I wanted her so much even though she was so drunk. As I lay next to her.

I washed her dirty clothes and dried them on the radiators while she slept in my bed.

It's all a while ago now. And I get up early every morning and go to my burger bar, drive the car, park it there, go to the cash-and-carry and stock up, fire up the grill, chop and slice meat and onions and vegetables, get the coffee machine ready, watch the cars and commuters in the morning light, long days, summer and autumn, in the evening light, I love the long dark winter evenings that set in so early, the smell of mulled wine and sausages, the last guests...

'You're still waiting for her, am I right?'

'No, you're not right, Mario.'

'You think she'll walk through the door one day.'

'No, I don't.'

'Come on, you do, just a tiny bit...'

'Mario!'

'Just a tiny weeny bit! Not every day, but now and then... often, right?'

'Leave me alone, Mario, what would I want from *her*...?'

'Come on, you can't fool me. You're waiting, aren't you? You're waiting.'

'Well, that's just the way it is sometimes, Mario.'

'Exactly. That's just the way it is sometimes.'

And just because I think of her, think of our evenings in the stairwell, of the light that stayed so long in the evenings, of the lights going out in the satellites, of me looking through the gap in the door to the women's section in the mosque, and of that one night, it's got nothing to do with the whole religion thing, or whatever you want to call it, being suddenly present again. What's the present anyway? Presence in the moment is a myth and a false idea, we're always in a different place, and I know what I'm talking about because I run a burger bar in a single-storey building with a roof projecting over it, which used to be a petrol station.

UNDER THE ICE

The first time I met him was at the airport in Vienna. It was one winter early in the 2000s.

I was on my way back from the Balkans, or to be precise: from the countries of long-collapsed Yugoslavia, where I worked for a railway company. We patched up the old lines but I wasn't patching up the tracks personally, I was in planning. Not the major planning, though, other people did that, I just coordinated the workers and the workflows and often went out to the tracks and the stations, destroyed years before.

He stood out the moment I saw him that first time, at the airport in Vienna. A short man, maybe five foot two or three. He was wearing a slightly battered suede coat with a fur collar and a checked flat cap, dark and shiny with melted snow because it had been snowing uninterrupted for days, but it looked kind of posh, expensive and 'very British', as we Germans say. Later on, when we were waiting in the little amusement arcade and playing the poker machines because the flight was getting more and more delayed, he told me he'd bought the cap in England, 'pure new wool, hand-sewn, only the best', in Newmarket, a town just for horses, as he said, 'thousands of English thoroughbreds', and he told me about his old cap (we call them *Schiebermützen*, pusher's caps – did black marketeers used to wear flat caps in the old days?), a hat he'd worn for over thirty years, 'I was sixteen, a present for my first win, that was in Gotha, the racecourse is on a hill there, Thüringen and the forests and an old grandstand from the Kaiser's days, the horse was called Wild Rose and we won by a length and a half, I know it off by heart.'

He'd been in front of me at the desk, trying to

communicate with a thickly accented Swissair employee, when I heard he wanted to get to Dresden on the same plane as me, although I was flying on to Leipzig. I immediately noticed his soft Saxon dialect in the midst of the loudspeaker announcements and buzz of voices around me, and I spoke to him and told him it might be a while because of the snow and the storms, I'd heard as much, and he nodded, looked me in the eye and said, lisping through his slightly wonky front teeth: 'Then we can wait a while together, later.'

It was one of those flights that put in a short stop before their final destination: unload a few passengers, load up some new ones, and then take off again. That always feels kind of strange at night, people getting off and vanishing in the semi-darkness of the airport buses, everything submerged in tiredness. The wheels would turn again, we'd lift slowly back off the ground... I often used to take that route later too, Vienna–Dresden–Leipzig, usually got to the airport far too early and played in the amusement arcade on my own, on the poker machine, and I'd send him a text message that he usually wouldn't answer until weeks later, but a couple of times he rang me back right then and asked how my game was going. Jack, queen, king... and then the ace came up and then the ten as well, he jumped up from one of those bar stools they put in front of the machines, and he yelled, 'I knew it!'

He rubbed his hands, pushed his cap to the back of his head and stared down at the machine, and I couldn't help being pleased for him, and patted him on the back.

'Usually,' he said, sitting back down on his stool and seeming almost embarrassed about his brief outburst, 'usually I don't bet on electronics, but sometimes...' he halted, sipped at his plastic cup of coffee, on the house, or on the amusement arcade and brought over by the staff, he sipped at his coffee and held out his hand to me, 'sometimes... Frank, the name's Frank, by the way.'

Later on, both of us started losing big, and he told me about the horses.

He'd been a jockey, a few years back, that was, and he actually wanted to fly via Zurich to St Moritz to watch the races there, but he'd missed his flight, the snowstorms had locked down the airports. He told me about the winter races on the frozen lake, the big Lake St Moritz.

'I've been wanting to go ever since 1989. And I'd saved up for this year. And now it's all fallen through. The horses give off steam as they gallop through the snow and across the ice, you've never seen anything so beautiful. I watch it every year, at the bookmaker's I mean.'

'At the bookmaker's?' I asked.

'In the betting shop, at our racetrack, where they show all the horse races. They're swathed in steam like little train engines, the horses I mean. And how they run, those long dark bodies in the white... and all around them the mountains, the Alps,' he moved his hands and the coffee cup in mid-air, as if tracing the lines of the mountains on the horizon, 'and there was a grey in one race, I made a killing on that one, at the bookmaker's I mean, and it looks, you get it, that grey, it looks so beautiful, I've always loved greys, sitting on those white backs... Mind you, there are people who don't like greys, they say they never bet on a grey. I used to know a grey once, I rode him a couple of times, his name was Chromat because he looked like he was coated in chrome, a beautiful horse, he was...' every time he said 'horse' he paused for a moment, 'a beautiful...' and hesitated, he'd spent his whole life with horses, I found out later, '... and that grey, in between all the other brown and black... bodies,' and he said it very softly, spoke the word almost tenderly, that *bodies*, and he looked at the playing cards flickering on the screen in front of him, 'and there, in St Moritz, it looked like the jockey was floating. You get it, like there was no horse, in mid-air, in the middle of the crowd of other jockeys, floating...' He nodded a couple of times, and the way he'd told me about it, I could imagine it well, barely hearing the machines' quiet melodies. Snow had fallen on the line near the Albanian mountains where we'd been working a few days before, and we dug the tracks free and wrapped ourselves up in thick coats, and as he told me about St Moritz I almost thought I heard the thunder of hooves on that iced-over lake, snow on the mountains, a race on a frozen lake, and the tiny clouds that the horses breathed out with a snort, and the steam rising from their sweating rumps, mingling with the snow kicked up by their hooves.

He was still staring silently at the screen, as though seeing his floating rider there in front of him, the white horse only visible in the whirls of snow when you looked carefully...

I pressed a few buttons, inserted coins, and out of the corner of my eye I saw him fumbling a cigarette out of a tin box and lighting it with difficulty.

'Isn't there a risk of them falling through?' I asked.

He blew out the smoke and waved his hand in dismissal. 'The ice is very thick. Minus ten or fifteen. Really cold. And they thunder across it so fast, their weight's only on one spot for a fraction of a second. Not even a minute for a thousand metres. And they have special shoes on their hooves so they don't slip. Nothing can happen, nothing's ever happened over the past...' he waved his cigarette to and fro in front of my face, the ash falling on the coloured buttons underneath the screen, 'almost a hundred years, I'd say, it must be by now. No, it's impossible. There's no way they can fall through.'

I wanted to ask him how he could be so sure if he'd never been to St Moritz, but he'd ridden himself, as a jockey, he'd told me that earlier, and jockeys are all pretty short, like him, that was almost all I knew about jockeys and racing, even though I'd been to the race-track in Leipzig a couple of times.

And I told him how my dad used to take me to the races in Leipzig back in the day when I was a kid, back in the East, and then I told him about the Balkans, or, to be precise, about the destroyed countries of old Yugoslavia, where we were patching up the broken train lines, and he nodded and said: 'Yeah, the world's come apart at the seams, everywhere,' and then we played a couple more silent hands on the poker machines, and then I went back to the desk but the flight was still delayed; the snow outside must have got even thicker.

The amusement arcade was slightly concealed between the cafés and the food outlets, *Melange* and *Sachertorte*, only a few people left in them, a turnstile behind the entrance, barely any light except the machines' coloured flashes, and there were only a few people in there too, inserting money into the flashing slots, and it took me a moment, once I'd gone through the turnstile, a man in a black suit standing next to the turnstile and nodding at me, until I found our corner, where he was still sitting staring at the screen, absolutely motionless and slumped on his stool, making him look even shorter, a dwarf in a glowing cave, when not long before he'd looked so alive, almost pleased, when I'd spoken to him, earlier at the desks.

'Just a few years,' he said, when we'd been sitting

there almost an hour, and by then it felt like we'd known each other for ages, the intimacy of amusement arcades, waiting and winter nights, Balkans–Vienna–Dresden–Leipzig and the ice on the big lake, 'I mean, you get it, only a few years later I'd have to have been born, maybe ten years or a bit more, about your age would be best, and then I could have ridden there, in St Moritz, on a lake; that was always my dream.'

I'd pegged him for late forties, early fifties, but sometimes when he talked about the horses, their names like magic spells, he seemed much younger, and he wasn't much taller than a child.

'These days, what chances I'd have these days... It's not just St Moritz, Paris-Longchamp, what a track, you can't imagine it, the best horses in the world, or Ascot, Royal Ascot, it all has majesty, you can sense the tradition. The Queen, and the Queen's gorgeous horses. And the huge grandstands, no comparison to Leipzig, Dresden or the Passendorf Fields in Halle, and wonderfully looked after. And the money, the prize money and the starting money they pay there, it's no comparison, no comparison, and tens of thousands by the side of the track and on the grandstands, cheering you on... Just a few years, you get it?' He sipped at his coffee, then he took off his cap and ran his hand through his grey hair. I saw that his forehead was wet with sweat. He put his flat cap down on the screen (later he told me he didn't like the word *Schiebermütze*, a *Schieber* was another word for a foreman, he preferred the name *Sportmütze* because he'd been working in equestrian sports his whole life) and he moved the checked sports cap absent-mindedly over the flickering poker cards.

'Whereabouts in Austria is St Moritz?' I asked.

'No,' he said, his smile revealing his wonky front

teeth, 'it's over in Switzerland. But I only made it as far as Vienna. My wife always wanted to come to Vienna. The old imperial stuff, coffee houses, *Sachertorte*, the Prater... Somehow, we never made it. And now I'm stuck here. No St Moritz for me, as per usual.'

He put his cap back on and pressed a few buttons and swapped three cards, which was no use. We were both on a losing streak by then.

I don't know why we didn't go to check-in and wait at the gate. They'd said it'd be at least two hours, and most passengers were probably upstairs by then and waiting and looking through the glass fronts at the gates, watching the snowstorm, frost flowers on the glass, but we sat in that gloomy little arcade and all that glittered there was the machines, playing their melodies now and then. The Prater fairground was closed at that time of year.

'Now, though,' he said, because he had four threes, and for a moment his earlier enthusiasm was back, 'now we'll get those coins jingling, though!' A four was worth thirty marks; Frank had put plenty of coins in the slot but now it seemed to be paying back at last. But then the machine asks you if you want to double your bet, at least take the chance. Red card or black card, fifty-fifty, not bad odds. Frank pressed Red. Doubled up to sixty. 'I'd say it'll give me red again.' A hundred and twenty. He was perfectly calm now, even though he'd been so happy before over his first win. 'But my wife never wanted to come to St Moritz with me. To the racetrack, I mean. The frozen lake. You and your gee-gees, she'd always say, isn't it enough that they're your work... Can't we just go on holiday like normal people?' He imitated his wife, wobbling his head as he spoke, and it made me laugh.

'She was probably right,' he said then, 'but the horses... they're more than just work.' He stared at the screen, thought about it, two reds in a row, another red now? Or black? Then he suddenly reached into his side pocket, took out a large mobile phone, looked at the display for a while as though someone had texted him a tip, then switched it off and put it back in his coat. Maybe he didn't want to be disturbed.

'And when you were there yourself,' I asked, 'on the horses, I mean, did you bet then?'

'Now and then,' he said, 'here and there, of course. Information, you get it, I was always up close to the right information. We rode the horses in training as well, so we knew what kind of form they were in. One time I came second in Berlin, at the derby that was, at the Hoppegarten track, and it was close, really close, a photo finish, we were neck and neck. Not a hand's width between us. Not even a head, not even a nose. I still think it was my win, still think that to this day. No matter what they saw on the photos. I'd put a whole lot of money on us, my wife grumbled all the way as she took it to the betting counter. Moonstone.'

'Moonstone?'

'Yep. That was the horse's name. I still think to this day, they just didn't want me to...'

'How often did you win in your career?' I asked, remembering how my father had taken me along to the racetrack when I was a kid. He didn't know much about racing but he was fascinated by the characters hanging around there, gamblers, horse freaks and huge crowds like at a fairground, and then the little jockeys he used to point out to me, standing there by the hedge in their brightly coloured shirts, some of them smoking cigarettes, and maybe a young Frankie was one of them.

'There were better jockeys than me. There were worse than me. I won in Warsaw once, in a preliminary race before the famous Wielka Warszawska. Dewdrop. That was my best season. Nearly fifteen years ago, now. Then I stopped, had a bad fall. My horse stepped in a hole, happens sometimes... That was my last ride. Wild Rose. I know that off by heart. A lovely mare. We had to put her out of her misery.'

He pressed a button, picked a card, red or black, fifty-fifty – wasn't the horse he won his first race on years ago called Wild Rose? – the card came down, he doubled his win to two hundred and forty. He nodded and looked at me, as if to say 'Easy peasy, isn't it?' and I said: 'Come on, cash in your winnings, empty the can,' but he wanted to double up again. He stared at the screen. Red or black?

'When a tendon rips like that,' he said as he thought about it, 'you can feel it before you go down. And you know that was it, for the horse I mean, and you try to roll off safely so you don't end up trapped under the body.'

'Did you ever break anything?' I asked, because he didn't look like he was going to hit either of the buttons, red or black, two hundred and forty. Was it euros or marks? But we were in Vienna, didn't they have shillings until the start of the 2000s?

'Did I ever break anything?' The short man laughed and took his hand off the buttons. 'I stopped counting. Collar bones, arms, shoulders, legs, ribs, I broke them all, all of them. Everything but my neck.'

He laughed again, but this time very softly, one of those bitter laughs that I often saw and heard from him, later.

'I was luckier than some of the other jockeys, though. But still, I broke everything, several times over. On X-rays... our skeletons look like trees.'

And he picked red again and I saw his hand trembling.

Only very slightly, at least I think so, looking back. Four hundred and eighty. Again, he didn't cheer and he stayed put on his stool, calm as though it was no big deal for him. 'Come on,' I said, 'empty the can, cash in your winnings.'

'There was this old ritual,' he said, 'when a horse died at the racetrack, when we had to shoot a horse. We'd go over and... but I don't think they do it any more.'

He didn't tell me what the ritual was, though, because the four hundred and eighty were gone. He'd tried out black but the damn can dealt him a red card. Or was it the other way around?

'Ah well,' he said, raising his hands, 'money comes, money goes.' But then when we walked towards the gates, the aisles empty and the only people we met tired cleaning staff pushing their carts past us, he did admit it would have been 'a nice bit of money' for him, and he stroked the fur collars of his old suede coat with regret.

'But, actually, it's fine,' he said a bit later as we walked on through the empty glass halls and aisles of the airport, 'because that,' – he pointed his thumb back over his shoulder as though the amusement arcade where we'd sat side by side for so long were behind him – 'machines, computers and all that, it's the end of the moonstones.' He smiled.

And later we went to the bar for a while, up by the gates. It was barely snowing by then and we saw them clearing the runways of snow and de-icing the planes through the glass front. When I offered to get him a cognac to go with his coffee, he turned me down. 'No thanks, I gave it up ten years ago.' He had put his cap down on the counter next to his coffee cup, and he tapped at the checked fabric.

'When they say, Frankie, go over to Newmarket for

the big auction and get us a good horse, I need to be straight. In the old days we used it for Dutch courage.'

He picked up my cognac glass, held it up to his face and looked through the amber liquid, then he put it back down on the bar.

I wanted to ask him who sent him to Newmarket, to the big auction, but then I didn't. What did it matter? He could fly to the town full of horses, and that seemed to be the most important thing for him. Dewdrop, Wild Rose and not red or black.

When he got off the plane in Dresden he waved one more time and walked across the runway, his body leaning slightly on the slippery ground, it almost looked like he was limping. It was barely snowing by then and I saw him vanish in the darkness as I sat on the plane behind the window. I had his phone number, a very short man in a checked flat cap and a worn coat.

It was night by the time I got off the train in St Moritz. I put my bag down on the snow, wrapped my scarf around my neck and pulled my shapka down over my ears, a gift from the stationmaster in a small town in Serbia, which we'd connected back to the railway network. He'd been living in the station for years even though no trains ran, old timetables piled up on the desk in his office, by the window overlooking the dilapidated platforms. The winter came suddenly and we broke off our work and got on with planning and administrating and waited for spring.

As the train pulled out, I saw the lake. Iced-over and covered in snow, it stretched below the station in a hollow, between mountains that rose in crags to the night sky – or were they clouds? – beneath which the lake seemed to shine, a huge flat white moon.

Then I saw the tents and booths, a grandstand of steel

tubes and crowd barriers down on the lake, all of it far off and hard to make out, dark shadows against the white background.

I turned around, picked up my bag and walked towards the station building, behind which the mountain ascended, lights of houses and hotels on the slopes. I took my phone out of my coat pocket and looked at the route to the hotel, which I'd downloaded from the internet. Back when I'd met Frank at the airport in Vienna, our mobiles still had pull-out aerials and huge buttons, but no internet connection. I stepped into the light of the station concourse and took off my gloves.

The hotel where Frank and I had reserved our rooms was only a few hundred yards from the station. We'd planned the trip the previous summer, when he'd visited me in Belgrade because he was delivering a gelding he'd bought off some Serbian horse man. 'It has to work out this time,' he'd said. 'St Moritz. I've put a bit of money aside.'

And that was a good thing because the hotel was really expensive, even though we'd booked it months ahead.

I walked along a path up the hill, lanterns lit on either side. The path was cleared of snow but it had snowed a bit more and even now a few flakes were crumbling onto my coat, and not much later more and more snowflakes were whirling in the yellow light of the lanterns, and the higher I got up the path, the thicker the snow on the ground ahead of me. I stopped for a moment and looked around at the brightly lit windows of the houses and hotels alongside me on the slopes, but there was no one about. I kept walking towards the hotel, looking at my phone.

We'd seen each other a couple of times over the past few years. He travelled a lot, like me.

He was head groom or stablemaster here and there, Dresden, Leipzig, Halle, had worked for a year at a racing stable in Dortmund, 'but I wasn't cut out for the West', bought and sold a horse now and then. He rarely talked about Newmarket, the town full of horses where he'd got his elegant sports cap.

'Are you still in the white city?' he'd asked on the phone, and then, although it was perfectly clear to me, he'd added: 'It's me, Frank, Frankie.'

'Let's go to the cold white lake at last,' he said then, later, in Belgrade, the white city where I'd been working for months, on the tracks destroyed at the end of the nineties. He spoke a bit of Russian and Polish, lots of jockeys came from the Eastern bloc, after 1989, '*beloye vino, da, da, da, beloye schnapps*, that was what they called our good corn schnapps, but I'd given up drinking by then'.

When he got out of the front of the horsebox in Belgrade, I noticed he was walking slightly bent, as if in pain. But he'd been driving the horse around for more than fifteen hours, and he'd limped slightly even the first time I met him, at the airport in Vienna – 'our skeletons look like trees'.

He held his left side, just below his chest, then he swayed his upper body a little and gave me one of his exuberant greetings.

'No, Mr Krause has not checked in yet.'

I didn't understand why she was speaking English to me, and I asked again, in German of course, whether he'd left a message for me, and the woman at the reception desk answered in English again, 'No, Mr Krause did not leave a message,' and I said, '*Sie können Deutsch sprechen,*' and she said 'I just speak Swiss German, I just understand a little bit of your Deutsch.'

Our hotel was in the shadow of a huge accommodation complex that rose out of the mountainside like a castle; I'd seen it even from the station.

I said, 'I go to the bar,' took my room key and went to the bar on the other side of reception. I felt like the woman at reception was dicking me about with her weird English.

But the whole show was kind of typical for Frankie, and for a good while I expected him to pop up somewhere, the man from Newmarket. But he hadn't been to the town full of horses for a long time by then.

'What kind of horse is it you've brought here?' I asked, pointing at his horsebox. We'd met up near the old Hippodrome; the stables were below a flyover that led into the town centre. The heart of the white city was up on a hill, and the Hippodrome, the racetrack, was down in the valley.

'Not good enough for our world any more, but fine for this one!'

'How do you mean, Frankie?'

'He was actually a goner. Damaged tendon. I pepped him up again though. It's only pin money, what they pay here, but still.'

'And he's been in the back the whole time?' I pointed at his horsebox.

'No. I let him out for a bit in Austria and took him for a walk in a field. Meadow kind of thing. He almost got away, the cheeky bugger.' He went closer to the box and stroked the metal, as though it was the horse's coat. A whinny from inside. 'See, my boy, we're here now. You know we're here.'

I sat down at the bar and drank red wine, but Frankie didn't come. I looked at the text message he'd sent me that morning. 'Don't worry if I'm late, tight change in

Zurich. Definitely see you at breakfast or at the race. On my way to the airport, see you soon, Frankie.'

I wanted to call him but then I didn't, just looked up on my phone when the last trains ran from Zurich to St Moritz. There were plenty of connections and some of them didn't arrive in the little mountain town until the early hours of the morning.

'You want to have another drink?' asked the woman, who had followed me from the reception to the bar and was now behind the counter there.

'Yes, please,' I said, and she poured me another glass of red wine. She stuck the cork back in the bottle and put it underneath the counter. It was a good red wine and it cost a pile of money, and when Frank got here he'd be glad he'd given it up.

He'd often told me about all the drinking the jockeys did. 'It's different these days. And we didn't all drink, of course. The worst thing was the bloody hunger. We had to make our weight, we had to be the right weight all the time. I could ride at fifty-three kilos. Sometimes even fifty-two. But then came my nerves on top of all that.'

We'd met after the races in Leipzig at the Alte Waage, a pub inside the racetrack, where the track the horses galloped along led right round us in a circle. He talked quietly, as though he didn't want the others to hear him. To hear about his nerves. The tables in the Alte Waage were occupied by trainers, jockeys, gamblers, racetrack staff, and most of them had said hello to him as we came in. He'd taken off his Newmarket cap and put it down on our table. But then he didn't say any more about his nerves. He did talk about his daughter, though. During the races we'd stood on the grandstand, on the other side of the track, right by the finishing line, and he'd sized up the visitors around and below us, during the races too,

147

as if looking for someone.

He'd been divorced for years and he rarely saw his daughter.

'She didn't come, again,' he said in the Alte Waage, 'even though I sent her a grandstand ticket.' He'd rested his hand on his checked sports cap and moved it to and fro on the tabletop.

'This is a nice *mitli* for the head,' said the receptionist, and stroked the shiny black fur of my shapka, which I'd put down on the bar next to my wine glass.

'Yes,' I said, 'it's mink. It was a present,' and she nodded and then went back over to reception. Presumably she'd heard a late arrival coming up the hill before I even noticed someone coming into the hotel. I stood up. But it was just a tallish, fat man with a wheelie case, and not Frankie.

'Your nerves,' Frankie said, 'if you ever take a really bad fall... or not *ever* – what can you do?'

'Your skeletons look like trees,' I said, and I watched Frankie and a couple of stable boys walking the gelding out of the horsebox. The horse kicked hard with his rear legs, and later Frankie explained that usually that only happened when they loaded the horses up. 'When they first go in, right, of course, who wants to get in a tin can like that? But we wanted to get him out, in his new home.'

But the gelding Frankie had brought to Belgrade, to the Hippodrome, seemed not to think much of his new home. He turned really stubborn when he was standing on the folded-out ramp and only had a few more steps to go. The new owner was standing next to me, a guy in a grey suit and a leather coat, smoking one cigarette after another and giving a running commentary in Serbian.

The horse trembled, standing still on the plank from

148

the box to the ground, but when Frank went up to him, he grew perfectly calm. The stable boys let go of the ropes holding the horse's head, let them hang loose, and Frankie went right up close to the huge body, the long neck damp with sweat, put his hand on that sweat-soaked coat and spoke calming words to the horse.

The red wine had made me tired and I'd gone up to my room. I could see the lake from the window. The mountains were dark and the peaks were jagged, there was no moon in the sky and everything was black and white.

And in the night, when dawn was already approaching, I went out onto the big lake with Frankie. 'When my daughter was little,' he said as we trudged across the ice, 'I used to read her the fairy tale with the horse's head. Do you know the one?'

'I can't remember it,' I said. Horses thundered across the ice beside us and the snow they whirled up enveloped us like fog.

'Blow, wind, blow,' he said, and I heard him laughing out of the fog.

'What?'

'Falada, Falada, thou art dead...'

'Is that from the fairy story, Frankie?'

'Yes.' Again, horses thundered past us – had the races already started? – and wrapped us in clouds of snow. I felt the ice shaking. 'They cut off the head of Falada the horse and nailed it to a door, and then it spoke all sorts of prophecies to the unhappy princess.'

'That sounds strange, Frankie, it sounds sad.'

But again, I heard him laughing out of the mist, 'Alas, alas, if your mother knew,' he seemed far away, no more horses on the lake, where had the horses gone that had just galloped past us?

'Frankie,' I called out, 'where are you?' I felt something, beneath me. The ice vibrated directly beneath my feet, not the way it thundered and shook when the horses galloped past us earlier, and when I looked down all the snow had vanished and the ice was like glass, and under the glass I saw the long bodies, very slowly sinking...

I opened my eyes and someone was whispering in my room, 'Blow, wind, blow,' and I was scared I'd see a head nailed to the door, but when I turned the light on it was all empty.

I drank a mouthful of water and went to the window. It was getting light already behind the mountains, and the mountains' shadows stretched dark across the snow of the lake, and the shadows of the craggy peaks seemed to point to the track, to the brightly coloured tents, the barriers, a grandstand built out of steel tubes... Later, when the races had started, I stood in front of the grandstand, by the barrier beyond which the snow-covered racetrack ran across the ice, heard the race commentator's voice, 'Fire Eyes ahead of Ocean Wind, now they're closing in, Fire Eyes and Ocean Wind,' people standing next to me and leaning on the fence and rooting for and applauding the two horses that had left the others a good way behind them, firing them on as they galloped neck-and-neck towards the finishing line, but for a moment it looked, as they turned into the home straight in front of the grandstand, as though only one horse was galloping there at the front of the field, because Ocean Wind was a grey, one of those almost white greys, and the horse was barely visible in the whirled-up snow, it seemed as though Ocean Wind's jockey was floating, just like Frank had told me back then in Vienna. 'We made it, Frankie,' I said, 'St Moritz,' and I wasn't sure he could hear me over the noise, and then we went to one of the tents to warm up and maybe have a hot drink. I didn't care whether Ocean Wind or Fire Eyes had won; I hadn't put a bet on. There was an Evening Star in the next race and I put a few francs on that one.

'What was that horse called again, the one you brought to Belgrade last summer?'

'Evening Peace,' said Frank, leading the horse into the stall. The stables were pretty run-down, like the whole of the Hippodrome.

'I doubt he'll find his evening peace here, though,' I said.

'He's a racehorse,' said Frank, 'what else can he do...?'

'Retire,' I said, but Frank didn't answer, closed the stall door and went out to the yard between the dilapidated stable buildings, the big concrete flyover above them, and sat down on a bench against one of the walls. An old, small man. I looked back at Evening Peace, now eating from his manger, his back legs enclosed in blue bandages, a horse come all the way from Germany to the white city to run in third-class races, and then I went out to Frank.

'One day,' I said, sitting down next to him, 'they'll tear all this down and build a shopping centre or new flyovers.'

'Maybe,' said Frank, 'but there'll always be horse races, somewhere.'

'As long as you bring them the horses,' I said, and I closed my eyes and felt the sun shining over the flyover onto my face, and I leaned my head against the wall of the old, dilapidated stable. From somewhere, I heard the high metallic sound of a hammer, probably a horse being shod, and I remembered sitting with Frank a few years ago, it must have been not long after we first met in Vienna, sitting on a bench outside a stable that was as run-down and dilapidated as the stables at the Hippodrome in the white city, in Leipzig or Halle, and him telling me about his work as a stablemaster, fewer horses every year, a memory within a memory, and there, on that bench against a cracked wall with the plaster crumbling off it, while the hammer went on and on hitting the iron, I understood his dreams of Newmarket, the town full of horses, of Paris-Longchamp, of a frozen lake in the Swiss mountains with horses galloping across it.

'His days are probably over,' Frank said, and took one of his roll-ups out of the tin he'd had with him even back in Vienna. 'He's probably done. But it should be enough for the races here. I've pepped him up, his tendon. What can I do? No money, times are hard.'

'Evening Peace,' I said. 'Nice name.'

'We even had a Peace Bringer once, in the early nineties.'

'Long time ago, now,' I said, and he nodded and leaned his head against the wall, which was pleasantly warm from the sun setting behind the flyover, and I thought of the broken railway lines we'd been patching up for years by then. And then he told me again, his eyes closed, head against the wall, about Dewdrop and Wild Rose and Moonstone and his photo finish in the Grand Prix for three-year-olds when he was a young jockey, a race no one I asked could remember.

I watched the jockeys vanishing into a tent after the race, popping out again before the next race began, their wet safety glasses pushed up to their foreheads, their breath steaming, the horses' breath steaming. The sky was clear and blue above the lake; it had stopped snowing that morning.

We strolled around between the tents and food stalls,

there was a big bar made of ice where you could drink champagne or mulled wine, we ate something, drank something, some of the tents were only for rich people with VIP tickets dangling over their fur coats, 'Look at that Nubian princess over there, Frankie,' but he only had eyes for the horses on the big white lake.

In the seventh race, a horse had a fall, and we saw the jockey trying to roll off in the snow. 'Watch out, Frankie,' I wanted to call out, but he got back to his feet by the barrier, on the other side to the spectators, and the horse got back up and trotted after the crowd of other horses towards the finishing line, Evening Peace, Evening Star, carrying its rear left leg slightly high so it didn't touch the ground, like something was broken, 'maybe ripped a tendon,' Frankie said, and as we were watching the races in the Hippodrome in the white city, he'd left suddenly.

'Wait a bit, Frankie, where are you going?'

He'd started limping again and pressing his hand to his left side.

'No,' he said, limping towards the exit, 'I shouldn't have brought him.'

'Who can tell?' I said when I was right behind him. 'Falada, Falada, thou art dead...'

'What?' He turned around. The horses were coming back from the track beside him, coated in sweat and bobbing and weaving and snorting, he was standing close up to the fence, and just for a moment, in the evening light above the Hippodrome, it looked like he was walking alongside them, walking with them. To the unsaddling enclosure.

I folded the flaps of my shapka down over my ears. It had grown cold in the evening. I walked back to the hotel, and the surface of the lake trembled beneath my feet and the ice crunched, and I could feel it slowly breaking, very slowly.

When I landed in Leipzig the next day, I took a taxi to his place.

I'd called him a couple of times from St Moritz but he never picked up.

An old woman came out of the building as I was looking for the right doorbell, 'F. Krause', and I walked in past her. I waited until she was gone, listened for sounds in the quiet stairwell and then went up.

His front door was ajar and later I kept wondering why no one had looked in through that door that had been open for almost three days.

I waited outside his flat for a while. Then I phoned him before I pushed the door open, and I heard his telephone buzzing inside the flat, ahead of me.

He was lying on the floor, behind the door. His body was strangely twisted; doubled up like that, Frank looked even smaller than he already was. He had his cap on his head, slightly out of place, and his hair looked very white above his yellow face.

I remembered my dream, the one I'd woken from with a start in the hotel room. He was floating between the horses, small and naked and doubled up in the water, under the ice.

I stood for a while on the threshold, looking at him lying there like that. He'd tugged at his suede coat, the one he'd been wearing at the airport in Vienna back then, he'd pulled it off the hook on the coat stand, and the battered coat was on the floor in front of him and he'd laid his head on the fur collar for a pillow. There was blood beneath his open mouth. Dark and almost black against the wooden floorboards. One of his eyes was staring at me. Perforated stomach, they told me later.

He must have tried to get to the door, had reached the

handle with his fingertips but not had the strength left to call for help. His travel bag was on top of a small chest of drawers.

'Frank,' I said, and I sat down next to him and closed my eyes. 'Falada, Falada, thou art dead...'

And then they came, that was how it was in the old days, the almost forgotten ritual that might never have existed, when a horse died. It took them a while to walk across the whole track, and then they formed a circle around the horse, the jockeys from the race.

They lean forwards, bow, doff their caps, press them to their chests and pause like that for a few seconds.

THREE

My photographer was waiting in Wolfen. He was standing outside the tumbledown station building with his back to me, taking photos. The click of his camera was audible on the empty platform. The photographer turned round to me, and again his shutter clicked in rapid succession, and I raised my hands in front of my face to ward him off.

Wolf-men had been sighted in Wolfen, and we walked through the station building towards the town. We passed construction machinery and scaffolding but the builders seemed to have knocked off for the day. Smoke rose above the allotments, a scent of burning leaves.

An old man sitting on a park bench told us about the open-cast mines in the lowlands around the town, gigantic craters where once excavators ate away at the brown coal like lindworms.

I had passed a lot of lakes on my way into the town. Perhaps the machines were still there, rusting away underwater.

Wolf-men had been sighted in Wolfen, but when we got to North Wolfen we waited in vain for our contact. He was supposed to show us a house on Chemical Worker Road where a man had tortured his wife for days, transformed into a wolf-man, and then leapt out of the window, vanishing in a nearby thicket.

We walked up and down Chemical Worker Road a few times but most of the high-rises were empty. My photographer took picture after picture of the decaying high-rise buildings, concrete cancer roughening the surfaces.

The editorial team had a theory that the advent of the wolf-men was related to the contaminated ground. The chimneys of the long-vanished factories had breathed fire over decades. Other people talked about the forced labourers who had died here and couldn't find peace and came back to haunt the locals. A child playing alone with a ball, throwing it up against a wall over and over, told us something about a crystal border, but we didn't understand, and when we went on asking the boy he ran away. A little later, a Volkswagen crawled past us, a couple of young men giving us hostile stares through the windows, and when my photographer raised his camera, I put my hand on his arm.

We walked to the Wolfen Busch, a patch of woods on the edge of town. We crossed the Fuhne, a boggy little river snaking through the lowlands.

We lost our way in the woods that had seemed so small as we approached them. Sometimes we thought we heard voices among the bushes and trees. In a hollow, we found a plastic bag of bones and offal. Flies swarmed around it and settled on the camera lens, and we crashed through the underbrush and sought our way back to the town. Wolf-men had been sighted in Wolfen.

The man laughed.

How could he tell, they kept asking him later. But the man had laughed. He'd seen it very well, it was a clear evening, and during that brief time before darkness suddenly falls, he had passed the old border in the 261.

He'd taken over the block train in M. late in the afternoon. He'd had a few days' leave and his last runs before that had been to D., block trains loaded with cars from the Transparent Factory.

He liked departing from M. As a child, he'd often stood by the tracks or on the bridges there, where the tracks ran underneath, watching the old steam engines, still in use now and then; he'd waited until evening came and spotlights lit up the freight station, had seen the giant cranes trundling back and forth on rails and loading containers onto the trains, the sounds of the freight station piercing the nights, that screeching and rattling, the squeal of metal on metal. His grandmother had lived near the station, the tracks running right behind the houses, the freight trains running almost through a canyon, brown wagons open at the top and full of coal or rubble, nets stretched over them, domed grey tank wagons with the word LEUNAWERKE on them, he'd learned about the Leuna Works at school, a factory as big as a town, flames above the tall chimneys and the nights as bright as day.

As he drove the 261 with the block train through the outskirts of M., he had seen his grandmother's house up on the embankment. She was standing by the window on the second floor, waving at him. 'Can I go to the bridge, Grandmother?'

'All right, but make sure you're back before dark.'

The block train wasn't particularly long, he tried to remember the details, he'd signed it all off an hour and a half ago, how many axles had there been? He had slept well, his wife had taken him to the train in M. that morning, she hadn't done that for a long time but it was a lovely autumn day, mild for October. They had strolled around the town centre, had an ice cream, sat on a bench by the fountain in the autumn sun. The evening was clear too, he accelerated slowly to a hundred, checked the clock, he was punctual down to the minute on the timetable, he had done the stretch often enough, they'd soon be passing the old border, nothing left to see, but it was funny, you could feel it somehow, the border, the distance, the difference. Even though most of his runs took him to the other side of the border, for years now. The station platforms looked different, the people standing there looked different... Even though the border hadn't been a border for twenty-five years now. 'Grandmother, will you bring me something from over the border?'

'What would you like?'

'A little locomotive, Grandmother.'

Every time, before he set off at the start of his shift, he wiped the instruments in the driver's cab down with a lens-cleaning wipe or a hygiene wipe, cleaned the levers and the wheel and the gauges. He ran the cloth very carefully over the plastic, over the glass, wrapped the wipe around the curvature of the handwheel and the small handles. The cab was usually clean but it seemed to him, once he'd finished his ritual with the glasses-cleaning wipes or wet wipes, that he'd always driven this train, that it was his train, his cab, his space, always had been. The workmates who saw him with his wipes would often laugh, but he was a good train operator, tip-top TO, his workmates would say, always on time, always prepared to take on extra shifts, and he hadn't had a day off sick since his training.

The sun had gone down in the red of the horizon but it was still light enough for him to see the countryside and the stretch ahead of him. They'd just passed through the former border station, there was no slow zone there but he could still tell the platform in front of the old station building was always empty.

The land was flat and they were heading northwest. When visibility was good in the long curve just before a stretch of allotments, rising on either side of the tracks, he could make out mountains far away. They must be the foothills of the Harz. He had driven this route so often that he didn't look this time to see if he could spot the distant relief of the mountains, resembling a ridge of hills in the onsetting dusk.

He reached for his thermos flask and checked the gauges; in a few kilometres, in the outskirts of B., he'd reduce the speed slightly. He loved these night runs. That was the good thing about freight. The work was often in the evenings and at night. He had driven passenger trains as a TO too, but he loved the goods wagons, axle after axle and hundreds of metres long, the freight in the wagons, the tons of freight, tons of steel, and just him all alone in the cab.

The coffee scalded his skin but he didn't feel it. It was just a tiny fraction of a second, perhaps less than that, and he saw the man laughing even though he was surely a hundred metres away, the long curve he was taking at just under a hundred – where did he come from? – the man standing straight as a rod and looking at him, not next to the tracks, or maybe he was, no, there were the allotments in the red dusk light, he couldn't remember setting off the braking procedure, and he didn't breathe, no inhaling and no exhaling, a screech, the squeal of the brakes, which he heard and then didn't hear, and then the laughing man was dead.

He felt it, and he felt everything. They were still moving. One hand on the switch for the electric brake, one hand on the wheel. He saw that he'd put it in position zero. No, first he'd pulled the emergency brake, which automatically operated the electric brake as well. All brakes brake. Position zero, emergency brake, electric brake, auxiliary brake.

He looked out at the allotments, saw that most of them were abandoned. Gardens gone wild. He stood up, his hands still on the wheel and the switch. The thermos flask was on the floor, the coffee steaming. The hand on the wheel was red. He sat down again into the silence.

His phone rang. 'No, no, I'm fine.' Sunset or sunrise. His wife on the phone. Evening again, the west was over there.

'Yes, I said I'm fine, the guys will take care of me, don't you worry.' He hung up. 'I'll call you again tomorrow. Don't worry.'

He had left town so he wouldn't have to speak to the man in charge of the TOs when something like this happened. Counselling. A doctor. And he was still sitting in the hotel room.

The coffee he'd called down for had gone cold. He put his left hand over his right hand. His phone next to the coffee cup.

He had opened the door and stood for a while in the open doorway. What a beautiful sunset. Small, crooked fruit trees. 'Suicide by train,' he'd said on the duty telephone, and given them the location. Small, crippled fruit trees in the dusk. Shortly before the town of B., somewhere beyond the old border. He had brought the block train with the 261 from there further northwest and then to the west, to its destination. He knew he had to go outside. He took the torch. He had to reach for it with both hands. He was included in the statistics now. It was extremely rare for someone to stand in front of a freight train. He knew plenty of workmates from passenger transport who... Counselling, doctor, statistics, suicide by train. The man had laughed, laughed right at him. He looked at the red clouds, the west, the east. His phone jangled. He reached carefully for the coffee cup.

He had gone by car, first to M. and then on to B. He'd never crossed the old border in a car. 'No, I'm fine. It'll be fine. Yes, you know, the company takes care of us, Deutsche Bahn takes care of us.'

He rarely drove long stretches by car. He'd got his driving licence over twenty years ago, while he was still in training. He usually took local or regional trains to his shifts. The only time he used the car was around town sometimes, so as not to get out of practice. 'The TO takes the train, of course,' his wife often joked. That wasn't it, though. He knew plenty of workmates who came by car.

He loved the big station in his town. It was where he'd started his training, over twenty years ago. He could rest on the trains, relax and find peace, strength and perhaps a few minutes' sleep before his shift.

He stopped by his grandmother's house. Noon, a day in November.

He stood by the low barrier, behind which the embankment fell steeply to the tracks. He sat in the cab of his 261 and looked up at the house; the tracks forked, the points were set, the route was free. He drove slowly, feeling the tank wagons behind his locomotive – how many axles? – that was how it had started, wasn't it, not having the facts at his fingertips, sudden gaps in his concentration... 'But make sure you're back before dark.'

'But you must see me, Grandmother, when you look out of the window, you can see all the way to the bridge. Will you wave at me?'

He walked down the road a little way, his grandmother's house behind him. A wall separated the pavement from the tracks. Every few metres, the wall was interrupted by a mosaic of holes, through which you could see the trains passing. Whenever he went to his grandmother's house as a child, he knew he was almost there when he saw that 'holey wall', as he called it, alongside the train.

He stood by the wall and looked through one of the holes. As a child, he had to stand on tiptoe. The windows of a passenger train. Very close by, and like mirrors. The judder of the axles on the tracks. He turned around and walked to his grandmother's house.

Spitting until his mouth was dry. Spitting from the bridge, over and over. Sometimes, when it was raining or when it was winter and there was frost on the wires, tiny flashes of lightning flared up at the contact with the locomotives' current collectors. And red diesel engines pulled freight trains, no flashes there, along the tracks underneath the bridge.

He turned around, looked at his grandmother's house again. The winter was far off still, no, no one was standing by the window and waving, and he wouldn't wave either.

Screeching under the bridge, rumbling under the bridge. 'Will you bring me something from over the border, Grandmother?'

It had taken him a while to find the track section.

Flat land; no sign now of the foothills of the Harz mountains, which he sometimes thought he saw from the driver's cab.

He had taken a few wrong turns, driven first along country roads and then over muddy field tracks. Had looked for the place with his phone and a map.

The allotment gardens were directly in front of him. He must be somewhere between the towns of H. and B. Where exactly was not all that clear at a hundred to a hundred and twenty, seen from the tracks. How long the braking distance was... he knew that, from his theory lessons, they'd talked about *that kind of thing*, how many years ago was that? Eye contact.

A signal mast, a few kilometres away, closer to B., had shown him the way.

He was next to the track now, the track where the laughing man had been standing. The allotments really were derelict and empty. The garden fences leaned towards the ground, half-sunk into the earth. Collapsed sheds, overgrown grass pressed flat by the rain. No, this wasn't yet the place. He stepped over the sleepers. He was here because the man had looked at him. He thought he heard something and he leapt off the tracks. One leg hit the track ballast, the stones moving as he sought a foothold, his other leg fell on wet earth and he slipped. He slipped and his hands grabbed the railway track. He was here because he'd seen the man's face. He looked at his watch, which had slid towards the back of his hand, he righted himself and stumbled and fell against one of the garden fences. And he lay at the bottom of the low embankment, his back and head against the wooden fence, as the 14.22 from M. sped past, the wind tugging at his jacket.

The track had been free again for weeks now.

Then he saw that it wasn't mud on his hand, it was rotten fruit, smashed apples, pears, a grey mush run through with red-brown threads.

'You have to help me, mate.'

'Help you how?'

'I need information.'

'The laughing man? I'm not allowed to say anything, I can't tell you.'

'I want to know his name.'

'Why?'

'His face... Oh, forget it.'

He watched the train receding, took the hygiene wipes out of his inside pocket and cleaned his hand, trying not to look at the viscous mess, his eyes watering, and he saw the glow of the rear lights in the long curve, blurred through the liquid. He got up and climbed back onto the embankment. Nothing to see on the tracks. What had he been expecting? But sometimes they forgot something. Sometimes they found a piece of bone or an ear, years later.

He wandered around the abandoned allotments as dusk fell. The sky full of dark clouds, nothing but fields around the allotments, and a thin line of red above the horizon.

And he kept looking at his phone, where the man's name was shown on the display. He had pushed and pushed his workmate until he sent him the name in a text message. And now he knew the name.

He had found the place, it must have been right here, the man must have been standing right here. The small, crooked fruit trees behind the fence. The autumn screams of the crows above the allotments. The hands on the switch and the wheel. One hand scalded. Tons of steel and freight in the tank wagons behind him. The beam of his torch on the axles. And between the axles, the man.

He stood in the playground, which was empty in the

beginning cool of autumn, leaned on the climbing frame and watched the house. He'd never been to this town far in the west of the country before, near to another border. Was that Holland on the other side? He wasn't sure any more. He'd often driven trains through the place.

The house was one of those beautiful buildings from the 1870s, four storeys, stucco façade, tall windows, stone pillars on either side of the entrance, but the plaster had gone grey, the roof tiles had gone grey – although the house had grown old gracefully, wasn't a semi-ruin like his grandmother's house in the town of M., where rain fell through to the upper floors and the plaster on the rear wall to the courtyard had almost completely fallen off.

He had looked at the doorbell panel. The name was there; he lived on the second floor.

White curtains in the windows left a triangle free in the middle, but he couldn't make anything out inside the flat.

Later, in the evening – he was now sitting on a bench on the edge of the playground – he saw light in the flat. A child was standing at the window. Short dark hair, ten years old perhaps, maybe younger, he couldn't tell whether it was a boy or a girl, and the child closed the curtains and then stood for a moment longer in the window, the drawn curtains behind him or her, and looked at him.

As he climbed the stairs the next day, just after four in the afternoon, he could still see that face. He had a room in a hotel near the station, even though he'd come to the town in his wife's car.

He'd bought a map; his phone was turned off.

'Come on, we'll walk together, we're going the same way.'

He slowly spelled out the boy's name, which was written on a small slip of card inserted behind a tiny transparent plastic window. All school satchels had the children's names written on them. 'We can play together.'

But the boy just ran away, even though he lived next door on the new estate. He had short dark hair and his satchel bounced up and down as he ran and hit him in the back of the head; he must have adjusted the straps too loosely.

He rang the bell on the landing outside the flat. He had bought a small bunch of roses, asked the florist to tie a black ribbon around the bouquet.

He rang again. He had waited outside the building until someone came, not wanting to explain anything over the intercom, but it had taken a good while until a delivery service arrived and rang someone's bell. He had slipped inside after the man with the parcel, said 'Thanks' and jingled his keys.

The door opened. The woman looked at him. She said nothing. He heard the delivery man in the hallway. She looked at him, both hands on the dark wood of the door. He raised the bunch of flowers.

He sat on the edge of the brown leather seat, drinking his coffee and looking around. She stood with her back to the sideboard, her arms crossed, the flowers set down on the coffee table.

A few photos in the wall unit, heavy lead-crystal glasses, and alongside it a bookshelf. He tipped his head and tried to read a few titles on the spines.

'And you're a school friend of... my husband's?'

'Yes, a schoolmate.' He put the coffee cup down on the table, next to the flowers.

He had asked for a cup of coffee, 'Might you have a coffee for me? I slept badly,' and then he was embarrassed, thought it was inappropriate, but they'd been standing silently in the hall when she'd asked him in after a while, and he'd thought about a hot cup of coffee all the way from the hotel to the house, had passed a few coffee places but knew he mustn't stop. She had nodded and gone straight to the kitchen.

And he hadn't really slept badly, he'd been sleeping very deeply since that night. He wanted to wake up from the dreams he'd been having, since that night, but he couldn't. He was in the driver's cab of his 261, he threw the thermos flask of coffee at the glass in front of him, because right behind the glass was the man's face, the head balanced on a body far too small, and the face and the head melted into a mush of rotten fruit as the glass smashed.

'We often used to play together.'

'In his hometown? He never talked about it much.' She went to the sofa and sat down. He took the coffee mug in both hands, drank in sips and watched her over the top of the cup. An attractive woman, early forties at most, dark blonde hair, shining very bright in places in the afternoon light cast through the window, as though it was going white in those spots. Her husband's hair had been almost black. She came from around here, he could tell by the way she spoke.

'How do you know he... He never talked about you.'

'A friend of ours told me.' He knew she wouldn't ask who the friend was. He put the empty coffee cup down carefully on the glass top of the coffee table, next to the bouquet, next to her hand, which she had put down on the roses at some point. There was a picture of John Wayne on the mug, from some black-and-white film; he only noticed it now.

'He... he loved Westerns,' his wife said.

'Ah, yes.' He picked the cup up again and turned it in mid-air, using both hands.

Don't say it's a fine morning or I'll shoot ya, he read.

'I'd better go. I'm sorry I came. I mean...' He fell silent.

What was he doing here? He looked at the window, the curtains leaving a triangle free, a high ceiling with stucco patterns, he saw the afternoon through the triangle, saw crows on roofs, saw the empty playground where he'd stood just yesterday, saw the evening behind the houses, saw the unfamiliar town. Nothing was right any more. He wanted to ask about the child but then he didn't. He stood up.

'Wait... please. I'd hoped you might be able to tell me...'

'I haven't seen your husband for years. We were children.'

She stood up too and took the John Wayne mug out of his hands and put it back down on the table.

'Please, sit down. What... what was he like as a child?' He could feel her breath; he smelled cigarettes.

And he told her about his schoolmate who hadn't been a real friend, he was in the other class, the parallel class they called it back then. He wanted to ask about the child but he told her about another child, one he barely knew. 'We went fishing a couple of times.'

'Fishing?' She smiled.

'There was a big lake, on the edge of town. A little train ran around the lake, a Pioneer railway. We often used to go on it.'

'A Pioneer railway?'

'Yes, run by the Pioneers. A little steam railway. Pioneers... back then, the border. He must have told you that.'

'Yes,' she said quietly, 'the railway.'

169

'I'm sorry,' he said, 'I... I didn't think.'

'No, it's fine. A railway for children.' She smiled. 'He always was like a big kid, until he...'

She stood up and went to the window, turned her back on him. 'I'd hoped you could tell me why he suddenly didn't come back.'

He looked at the pale green vase the flowers were in, the black ribbon alongside it. How long had he been sitting here now? No, it wasn't pale green, it was more of a blue. He blinked. His eyes were watering. The open-topped cars of the Pioneer railway, his head in the wind, the other schoolkids laughing, the boy who'd run away when he spoke to him sitting in the car in front of him, the piercing high signal of the steam whistle... white steam mixed with the dark, heavy smoke of the coal fire... 'Disappeared?' he asked.

'He always spent a lot of time in his cellar... but that wasn't it.'

She was standing by the window and he could see the glass misting over in front of her face. 'He... just left. Didn't go to work any more. Can you tell me where he was? For two weeks.'

'No.'

'Another woman? I was never worried about that. And then he wouldn't jump in front of a train. So far away.'

'Maybe he was in trouble?'

'No. No, we were doing fine. And why there, why so far away?'

'I'm sorry.'

'No, no, it's all right. I just don't understand it. And he was so cheerful when he left.'

'He was laughing.'

She turned around to him and for a moment he felt

like she knew everything, saw everything, the night, his 261, him in the cab of the 261, two children who had only spoken to each other a couple of times. 'Come on, we'll walk together, we're going the same way.'

In the hotel, he dreamed of the cellar. He had taken one of the tablets the doctor had prescribed, for *sleeping problems*. The doctor had talked about a dreamless sleep, but he didn't really dream, he was just back there.

He was in the cellar room, a model railway on a table, not an electric one, a clockwork railway on plastic rails, he'd had a similar one as a child. Around the railway there were little wooden houses, a real Western town, a saloon, a bank, further off a whole fort with palisades and a gateway, the little wooden gates were open and between the posts stood a man with a rifle. And now he realized there were little rubber cowboys standing all over the sheet of wood resting on two simple trestles, by the railway. He'd had exactly the same ones as a child and played with them, almost everyone had those rubber cowboys and Indians.

The Indians were attacking. They moved through a kind of papier mâché landscape, green hills extending beyond the fort. His schoolmate, who hadn't really been his friend, must have spent a lot of time down here. 'He always spent a lot of time in his cellar... but that wasn't it.' He reached for one of the cowboys; he could pick it up, they weren't stuck down like he'd assumed at first.

He saw the railway train he'd wound up running through the town, past the fort, six wagons, eight axles of passenger transport, four axles of freight behind them, round and round in a circle, the key turning on the side of the locomotive, and he sank down in the soft seat, heard the exhausted clockwork, heard it getting slower and slower like a watch, quieter and quieter, until

171

the locomotive came to a standstill...

The light of the ceiling lamp sometimes got weaker, flickered, brightened again, and he saw that the shelves weren't filled with boxes but with document files... and he wanted to get up and look in the files – what had the man kept in them?

An apparently random collection of newspaper pages, double pages, single pages. Front pages, small ads, politics and local news, sport, all sorts of things underlined and circled. He flicked through, reading. It was a strange mixture, what he read. The lunacy of the world, the decline of some country or other; on another page, obviously cut out with a craft knife, the trial of a man who had embezzled money, a double lottery winner; and then suddenly, circled with blue pen in the local news section, the opening of a hypermarket outside the town he was in, sitting in this cellar. The newspaper pages were from recent years, one double page only four weeks old. So he'd been sitting here four weeks ago, reading the paper, picked out that double page, looked at his little Western landscape. *Sirens Too Quiet, Town Must Update Warning System.* He had drawn a thin blue line next to that article, which was more of a note in the local section. What sense did it all make? As he put the folder back a business card fell out. *Office Rentals.* A phone number below it. He saw that the tools next to him on the table were a hole-punch and a stapler. A banging sound, a crash, the hole-punch pushed down with the palm of one hand, the stapler pushed down with that palm, BANG, BANG, BANG, the room echoed, paperclipped, stapled, hole-punched, BANG, BANG, BANG. Old platelayers hitting the iron wheels with hammers.

'Hello?' he called out into the cellar's silence. The light went out. And when he called again, 'Hello, come here,' because the laughing man ran away from him, the man ran even faster, the child ran even faster, along the narrow tracks of the Pioneer railway, a train steamed through the night, the stamping of the engine, steam rising from the little chimney, open-topped cars behind the locomotive, a man sitting huge between the children who didn't even come up to his shoulders, the squeal of the steam whistle, no, that was the brakes, screeching of brakes, piercing deep into him, decelerating movement, movement that never ended...

The first snow had fallen. He had called his wife. She had cried.

'Come home, please come back.'

'Yes. Yes, I will soon.'

A bus ran to Business Park West. At first, he thought he should have got off earlier because the town seemed to end here, snow-covered fields and wasteland, a few allotment gardens, but then hypermarkets showed up again, DIY superstores, low office buildings, loading yards with trucks in front of long ramps.

The river was a little way off but he could make out the loading cranes of the inland port. There were freight stations there, he knew that. A wide road that the bus took led around Business Park West, smaller roads and streets leading into it, flowing into the courtyards of office buildings, ending in giant halls with TO LET signs on them, at haulage buildings, warehouses, food markets, builders' yards, then building complexes that resembled piled-up portacabins.

He traipsed through the slush, the sky clear and the sun shining; it had snowed all the previous night. At some point, the child who would later be the man who stood on the tracks was gone. His parents moved house, a new school, he couldn't remember, they'd only spoken a couple of times.

Dirty slush was tracked all over the floor of the room. A desk. A chair in front of it. Nothing else. He sat down. The sun dazzled him and he rested his elbows on the desk and laid his head on his opened palms. The landlord would be back soon. He felt the clouds moving in front of the sun, and raised his head. He looked out over the business park, saw the bus he'd arrived on, no one outside, where had the landlord gone, before? Hadn't he said something when he'd asked him to leave him alone for a few minutes, as though he had to think over his decision on renting the space...? 'A friend of mine rented an office room here four weeks ago, I'm thinking of taking it over from him...'

He sat on his classmate's chair, a boy who hadn't been his friend. What had he done in this room? Between the white walls and the glass wall. As he went to stand up he saw that something was scribbled on the edge of the desktop. Barely legible, in pencil, already slightly smudged. He thought he could read his own name.

He stood in the light of the low sun – hadn't it just been noon? – and he turned around the building made of office containers, shadows wandering across the asphalt in front of him, large, crumpled newspaper pages blowing across the ground, he heard sirens somewhere in the distance, and into this sound, which got louder and quieter now and then, mixed the signal of a locomotive, the signal of his 261, getting louder and louder, higher and higher as if it came from the whistle of a steam engine.

The boy stood behind the holey wall, his head directly in one of the openings. He'd been waiting a good while now, but then he heard it. Hissing and emitting white steam, it stamped along the track. He pushed

his head further through the opening, the low sun dazzling him, he saw the shining wheels, the rotating con
rods. He laughed.

THE RETURN OF THE ARGONAUTS

They came from a realm of shadows that had formed over decades in the rear yards of the Coal Quarter, small factories with round, soot-blackened chimneys where pigeons perched when no smoke rose from the outlets, workshops, coal merchants, dilapidated buildings with small birch forests growing on their roofs, empty, decaying factories, passageways to the road and to the light, but the light outside was murky too; shadows lay over these yards where I'd met them many years ago, and as I returned to them now the sun was shining, and nothing fitted together any more.

I had got off the train at the main station and put my bag in a luggage locker, even though I was planning to go to my mother's place in the evening, she had made up my old bed – 'I've built your bed for you' – I had called her from the train but now I switched off the phone, put the slip of paper with the numbers in the inside pocket of my coat and went to the East Side, to the big station's eastern side exit.

You don't get a key these days, you don't have to pull a key out of the metal door these days, you just get a little slip of paper that pops out of a slot, a wall full of safes holding travel bags.

The concourse was filled with the clack-clack-clack of wheeled cases, the weekend travellers wheeling and rushing to their trains at my back...

Had they ever left the Coal Quarter? Now and then, they'd visited their half-brother, who they called their eighth-brother because he looked nothing like them, and who lived somewhere near Cologne. I'd seen him a few times when he visited his eighth-brothers and his mother in the Coal Quarter, a short, thin, bespectacled man whose head always seemed to bob to and fro on his thin neck. I remembered that H. had worked for his eighth-brother for a couple of months, he was running a furniture transport place in Cologne at the time and H. had often done removals here in our own town, he was a good removals man who knew all the tricks, used straps and belts, worked from his legs to protect his back, and knew how to stow cupboard after cupboard, more and more furniture mysteriously fitting into the far-too-small back of the truck; most people think all you need is muscle power.

They did have muscle power, H. and his little brother K., a bit less than two years younger, who was a bricklayer, or was training as a bricklayer when I met them.

Back then, we thought H. would stay in the big city in the West, but then he was back after a couple of months. 'Why should I stay in Cologne?' he'd said. 'I might as well shift furniture here.'

Had they ever left the Coal Quarter?

I'd met H. at the station one time, years before. I was reminded of it when I was standing by the little metal door earlier, the door with my bag behind it, and running my hand over the lock mechanism, but all that happened was a piece of paper popping out of a gap, a slip with a number code on it.

I couldn't remember where I'd been coming from or where I was going, or whether I'd just been strolling around the station as I do so often, watching the travellers. H. was wearing his uniform and his army backpack, he was on the way to catch a train to the barracks. I can't remember where he was stationed; it was only for a year. They'd exempted me for health reasons.

'Oi, mate!' he called when he saw me, and then he laughed so loudly that his laugh and his voice echoed beneath the arches across the platforms, pigeons flapped upwards, 'Oiiii-aaate,' and not much later we were in the pub next to the staircase that led down from the platforms into the ticket hall, drinking beer and a few shots of brown spirits until his train had departed without him.

Then we got in his car, which he'd parked in a side street, a tiny old dented Renault 5 with no MOT, full of those hanging air-freshener trees, and drove through the night without a destination, from here to there, the windows wound down, 'Let's go and see M., let's go home,' and when we'd almost got to M.'s place – he lived in the Coal Quarter too – we had to go back again because H. had left his army backpack in the pub and it had all his stuff and his papers in it. The backpack was gone but we found it in the end under a bench on one of the many platforms. It was empty but H. just laughed, 'Let's go and see M., the sky's so clear tonight.'

My old schoolfriend M., who had introduced me to the brothers, M. the friend of the stars with the big telescope on a tripod up on the roof next to a puny birch tree, M. who had led me into the realm of shadows, those rear yards of the Coal Quarter where strange people dwelled, like figures from legend, fairy-tale dwarfs, giants, accursed women, led me to the realm of shadows and nightmares... but when we were there, when we drank with them, we became part of those dark tales ourselves...

We sat at M.'s place and drank, and then we went up on the roof to his telescope and looked at the stars. M. knew all the constellations. We ran across the yard to wake K., who was asleep already because he had to get to the building site in the morning, but he just turned around in his bed, 'Leave me alone, you're insane,' and so we went on drinking without him, M., H. and me.

Castor and Pollux. The inseparable brothers who once set out with the Argonauts. In the constellation of Gemini. One mortal, the other immortal, that was how M. explained it back then, slurring his words. 'Who are the Argonauts?' H. asked.

'Crazy guys looking for something, thousands of years ago.' M. held onto his telescope tripod, pressed his eye so hard to the eyepiece I was scared it would push back into its socket, and that was how he looked out into space, at the constellations, at Castor and Pollux. Did he tell us all the stories of the Argonauts that night?

In the morning, the MPs came to pick up H. Everyone in the Coal Quarter hated the military police. They were police, after all. When they led H., still half-cut, across the rear yard, all the old grannies leaned out of their windows and yelled at the two MPs in their pale grey uniforms with the guns on their belts, and one old lady tipped her potato peelings out over them, no, more in front of them, and they trod on the potato peelings with H., and I trod on them later too, a rag-rug of potato peel. I ran to the yard's entrance, to the road, but the MPs and H. were gone.

I blinked at the midday sun and left the station behind me and walked very slowly along the narrow streets to the East, to the Coal Quarter.

I sat down in Inge's Corner, where we often used to go. I wanted a drink before I rang on K.'s doorbell. He was back at his mother's place now.

Inge's Corner had got smaller, shrunk down.

At first I thought it was just my memories misleading me, an endless bar full of people drinking, their voices making the room even bigger, a dome of voices and sounds, the room getting larger and larger, mists wafting above the tables, flushed faces moving in the mist as though distorted through optical lenses, rolled-up shirt-sleeves revealing strange tattoos, glasses of all sizes on the tables, playing-cards floating through the air as if in slow motion, a fug of beer and sweat and grease, Inge used to cook herself back then and there was hot food round the clock, a smell that mixed with the fog of the cigarettes, and outside the chimneys puffed out smoke. The coal merchants did good business until the old buildings got done up or torn down and the coal stoves gradually disappeared, the coal merchants gradually disappeared, the Coal Quarter gradually disappeared.

Inge's Corner had shrunk down, a new wall put up through the middle of the taproom, and the big kitchen Inge used to bring trays of food from was gone too. I could tell by a sign behind the bar that they only served sausages with buns. And only a few people were sitting at the few remaining tables, the smoke of an occasional cigarette dispersing thinly into the room... What was behind the wall? A storage space, a flat? A shop? I got up and went outside to look at the building properly and solve the puzzle of the shrunken space, and as I turned back to the bar just before the door I saw a soldier sitting there, must have been there all along. In uniform, his beret rolled up next to his beer, next to a shot of brown spirits. He looked at me briefly, I nodded at him, and he raised his shot glass and drank.

It was cool outside, the sun setting behind the buildings. The Inge's Corner sign wasn't lit up yet, and it didn't light up later, once it got dark. I looked up the wall of the building. They'd done up the whole street, years before. But the plaster was beginning to go grey again, peeling in places, already weathered, damp creeping out of the ground into the brickwork – weren't there even

180

a few little birch trees growing on the roof? – I tipped my head back further, clear blue summer sky, the house went on slowly going grey, weathering as though it felt uncomfortable under all the new plaster, the houses had all been grey and almost black in the Coal Quarter, and they were going grey again now, even though the coal merchants had disappeared.

The brothers H. and K. – their father had been a coal merchant, they were rich and influential, the coal merchants, back when thousands and thousands of coal stoves puffed smoke into the sky... When he died he coughed as if he wanted to expel all the dust of those years, coal dust, mountains of coal dust that they'd put in the sacks and weighed along with the coal, dust that mixed in with the smoke of the chimneys, the factories, the cigarettes, dust that he coughed up when he died, H. trying to bring him back, H.'s hands on his chest.

'Where were you then?' his little brother would ask me later, the hour of the Argonauts, 'where the hell were you back then?'

Standing outside the building, standing in front of Inge's Corner, my head still tipped back so far it was hurting my neck, I saw the scaffolding in front of the façades, the scaffolding growing up to the sky, winding around the buildings, the birch forests on the roofs getting chopped down, we're standing on the scaffolding planks, H. and me, we work on building sites when we need the money and when H. doesn't pick up any removals, his little brother the bricklayer gets us jobs, we're builder's mates, labourers, shaft workers, gutters, the demolition brigade... We cough dust, red brick dust sticks to our tissues like nosebleeds, we wear mouth guards like doctors in surgery, we call the protectors 'Laddie' and the huge hammers we use to tear down fireplaces and whole

walls, we call 'Rover', we lug cement sacks and plasterboard up stairs and down stairs, we grip pneumatic hammers, our bodies vibrate, we yell into the noise, the old grey plaster leaps off the bricks, the façades, the walls of the buildings, thunders down the inside of the scaffolding onto the road, onto the pavement, dust rises, we stand on the roofs of the Coal Quarter wearing yellow helmets, they too are coated in dust, we see M.'s telescope, still on its tripod next to the puny birch tree, they haven't got that far yet even though M.'s gone now...
No, he was standing up there as H. and I worked on the roofs, the roofs of the Coal Quarter and the roofs of the town, he waved and looked at us through his telescope, the times are mingling together, it's grown cold, no light in Inge's Corner – when did M. disappear? – when did H. disappear? – when did I disappear? – death was on the prowl in our buildings, in our yards.

'Will you get me a drink in?' the soldier asked. He was no longer there when I opened the door to Inge's Corner again – had I been away so long, outside so long? – but then I saw the rolled-up beret next to an empty shot glass.

'Will you get me a drink in?' he asked again as he stepped out of the little gap in the wall that led to the toilets, despite the loss of space, and I said, 'What'll you have, mate?' I looked at him; he was at least ten years younger than me, hard to say exactly, but his eyes looked old and tired.

'The same as you're drinking.'

I looked at the bottles on the shelves behind the bar, just a few sorts of spirits and liqueurs, like in the old days, clear schnapps, brown schnapps, Castor and Pollux, H. used to prefer brown spirits to clear, he laughs and raises his glass to me, an endless chain of small glasses full of that brown schnapps moving around his head, glinting dully in the pub dusk... The landlord was somewhere in the bar room with the few drinkers, Inge had disappeared years before, sold the place while I was still living in our town.

I turned around and called out into the room, 'Two beers, two browns.' 'Coming,' the landlord called from somewhere. The soldier pressed his beret together with both hands while the landlord got our drinks.

I looked at the soldier but he seemed to be looking through the walls... H. had almost always been behind bars during his national service, had looked through the walls there because he'd punched his sergeant with his removal-man coal-merchant fist and because he often missed the train after the weekends.

'Two beers, two jokers.' The landlord put our drinks down on the bar. The soldier pulled the glasses over and raised the shot glass, and I waited for him to say something, to drink to something, but we drank in silence. No toasts.

'Where did you do service?' the soldier asks, putting his empty shot glass down slowly.

'I didn't do service,' I said. 'Flat feet.'

He nodded. 'Probably better that way. Will you get me another?'

'Did your pay come late?'

'No.' Now he looked at me and I knew that look, knew it from the pubs and bars in the Coal Quarter just before insanity broke loose, H.'s little brother K. often used to have that look, his pupils got smaller and smaller and then bigger again, like his eyes were breathing in and out. 'All right, soldier, why not?', a white glow, and behind that glow waited insanity, waited war, waited the first blow, K. slammed his glass into some guy's face, some guy or other who'd been annoying him for minutes, blood ran down skin, someone hit out at K., his brother turned up and punched some face or other, glass smashed, someone yelled, someone laughed, I stayed put on my seat and there was a strange calm in me, I sensed the way it all felt inevitable, the ticking-over of ancient rituals, old and older than the Coal Quarter, it was a realm of shadows, the walls dissolved and I could see into the flats, saw the old grannies sitting silently at their tables, saw the drinkers lying trembling in their beds, saw M. leaning over a book, the ancient myths and the stars – when had he disappeared, and why had he disappeared? – and I saw H., dancing with his girlfriend all alone between the tables and chairs, their bodies touching, his head on her shoulder, some old nineties hit playing, was it here in Inge's Corner or in one of the other Coal Quarter pubs?

And the soldier drank again. 'Was pretty dusty *out there*, eh?' I said, and he nodded.

'Still is,' putting the shot glass slowly down next to the empty one from our first round. The landlord went to clear it away, reaching for it, but the soldier said, 'Leave it, it looks nice like that.'

And the soldier drank again, three small empty glasses in front of him, three small empty glasses in front of me. I turned for a moment and called out 'I'll pay now, then.' The landlord was back at one of the tables, drinking with one of the few punters. His shot glass shone green, peppermint, that was what the old drinkers drank when their stomachs couldn't take any more hard spirits.

'I guess you're not from round here, mate,' said the soldier. 'I've never seen you in...' He halted and ran his forefinger through the air, drew a semi-circle around his face, drawing the Coal Quarter into space like a

184

one-handed conductor.

'I've been away a long time,' I said, 'I used to spend a lot of time here, in the old days, had good friends round here.' I touched the three empty glasses, which I'd pushed close together.

The soldier nodded. He took a squashed cigarette pack out of the inside pocket of his khaki jacket, pulled out a crooked cigarette, which he carefully stroked into shape and tapped on the bar a couple of times before he put it between his lips, then he put the box down next to his rolled-up beret. He was looking at the wall behind the bar again, seemed not to be paying me any more attention. But once I'd paid and gone to the door, he said – and his voice sounded strangely dull because he didn't turn around to the door but spoke to the wall instead, his words bouncing off it through the smaller room of Inge's Corner – 'Come back soon, mate, I'm always here.'

I woke with a start. It was dark and cold. I was sitting in the little park opposite M.'s house, actually just a patch of grass with a kids' playground. I looked at my watch. Only six. I had dreamed of the soldier. He didn't take a squashed cigarette pack out of his uniform pocket, it was a stable one, firm, and in my dream, it seemed beautiful, white, a white glow with a red triangle, what a gorgeous red, I wanted to touch it, the white and red, in my dream. The death warning was printed on the box in some foreign language, so I couldn't read it. And the soldier said, 'They make our poisons pretty beautiful, don't they?' It wasn't until my dream that I saw he was wearing a medal on his uniform jacket.

The windows in M.'s building were dark, probably no one lived there now. It hadn't been done up and they'd torn down a few buildings a bit further along the road, I could see the empty lots in the darkness and a bit behind them the big road leading out of town, lights moving there, red and yellow, that was the world of fast lights, the world of streams and networks. Was the telescope still up on the roof on its tripod? M. the friend of the stars, who knew all the constellations and told us stories when we sat with him on that roof. Castor and Pollux and the Argonauts. 'Go away,' he said to me, 'try something new somewhere. You're one of the clever boys.'

'Hey, hey,' I said, 'we're the same age! And what about *you*?'

He smiled and adjusted his glasses. 'Me? I'm doing fine right here.'

The bench I was sitting on felt damp and cold. I got up. K.'s mother lived a few doors down. I stopped by M.'s front door. The names on the bells were barely legible now. I put the palm of my hand on the bells, wanted to press them all but then I didn't, just stood there, stood for a while in the dark entrance to the yard, one foot on the stone threshold, my palm on the bell buttons.

She opened the door. She didn't recognize me straight away, and then she hugged me. She almost fell as she did, letting go of a walking stick. 'Come in.'

I bent down, picked up the stick and handed it to her. She limped through the flat ahead of me.

'K.'s not here,' she said once we'd sat down in the living room, her on the big couch, me on one of the armchairs. The ashtray on the coffee table was full of butts, one still smoking. An open can of beer and a half-full glass next to the ashtray.

'Beers in the fridge if you want one.'

'Yes, thanks.' I got up again. I'd almost forgotten, after all the years, that I was a friend of the family. On the way to the kitchen I passed the wall unit. In the cabinet, between glasses and china figurines, was a glittery black briquette with a gold-framed photo on top of it. She and her husband. The coal merchant, the coal deliveryman, the king of coal, the king of the Coal Quarter, the father of Castor and Pollux. He had his arms around his wife, who was now coughing behind me. On either side of the briquette were photos of her sons. Behind the briquette, a photo of a field of graves leant against the back of the cabinet. It must be somewhere outside of town. I went down the hall to the kitchen.

The door to K.'s room was there, the room the brothers had shared until they moved out and then back in and then out again. Where was K.?

I was scared of what his mother would tell me. I squatted down for a while in the light of the open fridge, then I took out a beer and went back to the living room.

'He always said you'd come back one day.' She'd leant her crutch up against the sofa, smoking and taking sips from her glass.

I wanted to ask if she meant H. or his brother. But I just opened the can of beer, a bit of foam spilling onto my hand.

'He's in hospital,' she said. And again, I didn't know exactly which brother she meant. H.'s time in hospital was long gone, but she lived in a realm of shadows.

'What's... what's the matter with K.?' I asked. And again, I was afraid of what she'd say, their mother. Had H. come to fetch his brother? Castor and Pollux, the inseparable brothers, like old women sometimes did with their old husbands, or the other way around...

I tried to remember... What had I felt when I heard first about H.'s, then about M.'s disappearance? I didn't come to town, not then.

It was an old world slowly disappearing, and its inhabitants disappeared with it. The Coal Quarter with all its odd people, like figures from legends and fairy-tales... Famous drinkers who got thinner and frailer like that Phineus M. told us about, an old man wasting away on an island, punished by the gods, and in the end all they could drink was peppermint liqueur and they'd do terrible things to each other on the drink, coal merchants who couldn't sell coal because the stoves were no longer burning, faded tattoos on old skin, old grannies with elbows on faded cushions, looking out of the window all day long, kids who lived in the pubs like their fathers and sat in the rear yards by night, sat on the kerb and drank, moved out and back in again, death was on the prowl in our yards, in our buildings.

'What's the matter with K.?' I asked again, because she hadn't answered; perhaps hadn't heard me. Or she had answered and I hadn't heard *her*. She had taken some tobacco out of a big tin and crumbled it into a kind of cigarette-rolling machine.

'It's... not his body,' she said and she lit the finished cigarette. 'It's his mind. He doesn't understand things any more.'

'Things,' I said.

'Why you never came. Why he's all alone, why his brother's gone, and M., you remember M., don't you?'

'Of course,' I said.

'Of course,' she said and reached for her cigarette from the edge of the ashtray.

We were sitting on the roof, only the tripod left without the telescope next to the half-parched birch tree.

'I come and go,' said K.

He was sitting next to me, his legs dangling in the darkness where the roof dropped off steeply to the rear yard.

'Oh, no, not that,' said K., and I could almost feel him

188

dangling his legs, moving his feet up and down like a kid, 'not that. That wouldn't be OK.'

'No,' I said, 'it wouldn't.'

'He just went yellow,' K. said, 'just like that. I took him to hospital... He couldn't...'

'And you?' I asked.

'...couldn't walk any more. Down there...' he pointed down into the darkness of the yard. The light of a half-moon, somewhere above us, behind us, only sparsely illuminated the roof, and the clouds covered it and migrated, and the shadows moved, and nothing fitted together any more; his father, his brother, M.

The building's front door I'd stood outside just earlier, my hand on the doorbells of those long-uninhabited spaces – K. had kicked it in, he'd been there suddenly when I walked across the rear yard of his mother's building to the passageway, he'd been standing in the passageway to the road, right by the wall so I couldn't see him at all to begin with.

'Oi, mate,' he'd whispered, and in the close, dark passageway his hoarse whisper had echoed strangely, 'Oiiii-aaate.'

'I come and I go.' It was only now I felt my hand was still on K.'s shoulder. It moved as he spoke.

'What do I want in those white rooms?'

'Don't they treat you well?'

He laughed quietly. 'Everyone treats me well.'

'I'm sorry,' I said, and I took my hand off his shoulder.

'Don't be, what for? I always knew you'd come. He can't walk any more, we have to get him out of here.' He moved his legs, properly swinging them, his feet briefly coming into view in the light of the half-moon.

'And M.?' I asked.

'Our good friend M.' Suddenly he was all there again,

189

perfectly compos mentis, and he turned and looked at me, his eyes looking old and tired, no clouds across the half-moon.

He had kicked in the door downstairs and it seemed to me, as he slammed his foot against the dark wood of the door, as though it would open before the wood splintered, before his foot kicked the door off its hinges. Castor and Pollux and the Argonauts.

'Once H. was gone, all M. did was sit up here. All we did was sit up here.'

'And he...'

'Once you were gone, all we did was sit up here. No, that's not true. You did come and you gave that nice speech. Over there, outside of town.'

'Yes,' I said, 'I did.'

'Yes, you did.' He leaned back, let his upper body fall back onto the damp roofing, a few moss-covered tiles still dotted here and there. I hadn't been in town, back then. I'd heard about their disappearances but I didn't want to come back to the Coal Quarter, I just couldn't do it, and I'd only seen their disappearances in my dreams.

'He went yellow. Overnight. Just like that. Stomach, liver, gall bladder, who knows?'

'And then he...?'

'They said only old men got it. It was like a miracle that he had it. He was too young, you get it, too young to go yellow just like that.'

I leaned back, lay down next to him so I didn't fall off the roof into the dark of the rear yards. I looked out across the roofs. Somewhere out there was the station where I'd just arrived, and around the station and so far away was the flicker of the town, which seemed to be a different town, and the tenements in the Coal Quarter were dark satellites.

'What did he call him, that skinny old man? Phineus?'

'You mean M.?' I asked.

'Yeah.'

'Yeah, those were his stories,' I said.

'Can you tell what anything is up there?'

We looked at the stars. 'No,' I said. 'Maybe the Plough.'

'There was this woman once, well, I wouldn't say a woman...'

And then he told a story about a toolbox on Phineus's island, and M., there for some reason, confused and alone, and Phineus and his friends and the woman and the toolbox full of tools, but I didn't want to hear it, the dark bad fables of the Coal Quarter.

'In and out,' said K., 'in and out.'

'What can you do?' I said.

'Drink peppermint,' said K., 'fall down.'

Then we stopped talking and lay on the roof and watched the half-moon setting.

After a while I went to my mother's. 'I've built you your bed.' My bag was still behind the metal wall of safes but I couldn't fetch it, didn't want to fetch it either that night. The slip of paper with the numbers on it was probably by the birch tree, by the tripod, where I'd sat with them one last time, the return of the Argonauts M. had always told us about. And they really were up there with us, on the roof.

K. had dug up both caskets full of ashes and put them in one of the chimneys, up on the roof; he hadn't told me when: months ago, years ago, days ago. I'd looked at him and I knew straight away they were really in there, knew he'd 'brought them home', as he called it.

They came from a realm of shadows that had formed over decades in the rear yards of the Coal Quarter, small factories with round, soot-blackened chimneys where pigeons perched when no smoke was rising from them, workshops, coal merchants, dilapidated buildings with small birch forests growing on their roofs, empty, decaying factories, passageways to the road and to the light, but the light outside was only murky too; shadows lay over these yards where I'd met them many years ago, and as I returned to them now I realized it had all disappeared long ago and yet would always be there.

He was quite calm as he took the last steps.

He thought of how he had roamed the land many years ago with an old Jewish pedlar. What had become of him? Had he taken his last steps somewhere too? He could not remember the old man's name. What had the old pedlar said to him, more than once? 'Greed, falsehood and cruelty rule the world.'

The old man had seen a great deal on his travels around the land. And he had told him a great deal, but he had not wanted to believe him back then. Not yet. Sometimes they heard the bells tolling, far across the land.

In a strange way, the old Jew had believed in Jesus, who had preached to love thy neighbour and thy fellow man, peace and justice, help and compassion, and he called him the first communist.

What does that mean? he had asked the old pedlar back then, because that word did not seem to fit into their time.

He felt a hand heavy on his shoulder. No, he would not go down on his knees. The block was in front of him. The wood was dark with blood. They forced him to his knees.

He asked himself, as he looked at his fellow travellers, standing behind the block in silence as they waited for their last steps, whether everything had not been in vain.

The struggle. The hatred for the increasingly unbearable yoke. The blood that was a different blood to that which had stained the block black. We were the just ones!

He wanted to call something out, pull himself together

and speak to the people who had come in droves to see... But now his mouth was suddenly dry and his voice was hoarse and rough, silenced forever. 'God's friend and all the world's foe!' he had shouted earlier. And because that was meant only to scare his foes, he did not believe in that God any more, he had added in an even louder voice: 'Foe to the rich, friend to the poor.' How would he be remembered in the distant future?

Willi Bredel read that last sentence over and over, then he put that page with the other pages, densely written on both sides, and stood up, resting his weight on the table. 'Klaus, my friend,' he said, 'what will become of us?'

Then he picked up the page again and his pencil and started scribbling notes and comments between the lines, writing over the words, here a cross in the margin, there a question mark or a squiggle that he didn't understand himself, 'three *had*s in a row,' he said, 'that's not exactly hat's off, had-had-had, but if it doesn't bother you, old friend...' And he pushed the page aside and it fell to the floor, and he threw the pencil down on the other pages fanned out across the table in front of him, then he sat back down. *Had roamed – had become – had taken*.

The light flickered. A bare bulb above the desk, the light inside it flickering.

He looked up. Sometimes, after hours of writing, he forgot where he was. Then he saw the rows of books, the shelves up to the ceiling, the aisles of books.

The city above him was dark now. No window was lit up, the streets were empty, the lamps extinguished. Soon the sirens would set in. He hadn't slept properly for days. Often, he woke up down here, his head among his papers. What was the point of going home? His wife was waiting for him. But the enemy was approaching.

His nation was approaching. The armies were approaching. The fascist was coming.

No, not his nation. His nation was here.

'We won't get old, Bredel,' his friend Becher had said just a few days ago.

And Willi Bredel had grabbed the thin man by the shoulders with both hands. 'We will win, you hear? We survived the camps, we survived Spain... We will win out!'

'We survived the camps,' his friend Becher repeated and looked at him out of tired eyes, 'we survived the hotel...'

'Shh... shh,' said Willi, as if comforting a child. 'Comrade, comrade!'

And Becher, who had never been in a camp (but Willi Bredel had meant that *we* as a reference to the nation of the oppressed and persecuted), Becher sank feebly into Willi Bredel's arms.

'Shh... shh,' said Willi and held him, 'don't you believe we'll win?'

'Of course I do, of course,' Becher said quietly, resting his head on his friend's chest, 'but we won't grow old. I sometimes think my heart is made of paper.'

Willi Bredel bent over the sheet of paper and tried to pick it up off the floor, but it kept slipping away from him and in the end, he crumpled it in his fist and picked it up. A stabbing pain in his head, a stabbing pain in his chest. Cautiously, breathing heavily, he straightened back up. Laid the hand with the paper on his chest. The light above him flickered.

Had he not heard the first distant rumble? The light went out briefly, and in the darkness, he felt himself stop breathing and listen into the dark, then the wire encased in the bulb's glass began to glow red again, grew brighter, and the bare bulb's flickering light illuminated the desk and the shelves and the books.

He had loved the Lenin Library ever since he'd moved to Moscow. Never before had he seen such a huge collection. When the enemy came, the committee had charged him with evacuating the most valuable items into the library's spacious cellars.

He had always loved libraries. As a child, he'd been to the workers' libraries, lost Hamburg, had gone to the school library, stood in front of the shelves and run his fingers over the spines, had read for days and nights during his turner apprenticeship at the factory, the workers' reading circle, man's fate, over and over again, his fingers on the spines and between the pages, his hands on the turning lathe, what on earth was it all? the dream of the new man. (He remembered the book by that Frenchman he had met in '34 at the writers' congress in Moscow, wasn't it called exactly that? *Man's Fate*. He remembered the hero being burned at the end by the counterrevolution, burned alive in the boiler of a locomotive. China. It was all far away and yet they belonged together. Man's fate. They had seen each other again in Spain.)

Sometimes, when he fell asleep, his head on the desk, on his papers, he dreamed of the books among which he slept. They were burning. And the strange thing was, that didn't scare him in his dream. He'd sit there, in the midst of the flames, and recite everything he'd ever read. And he smoothed out the sheet he had just picked up off the floor. And he read his last sentence again. And felt that something wasn't right. And, of course, it was right after all, that sentence. *How would he... be remembered?*

But Klaus hadn't been alone. It ought to read: How would *they* be remembered in the distant future?

Klaus Störtebeker, his old friend the pirate. Whom he'd met again in the rooms and the cellars of the Lenin Library. In the old Hanseatic city chronicles. Foe to the rich, friend to the poor.

In lost Hamburg they had played at being Störtebeker, in the back yards, around the port. *Pirates, bandits, democrats, which of them are dirty rats...* The tall, steadfast captain of the Likedeelers, who beat the patricians, no, almost beat them, 'Greed, falsehood and cruelty rule the world.'

But Klaus was alone as he walked to the scaffold. Was forced to his knees. As he laid his head on the blood-blackened block. Every man dies alone, no, no, no. What was there, in his last seconds?

A look, looks, thoughts and memories in his brain, which would soon disappear entirely. Divided. Severed.

He tried to remember what he had thought, during his last steps, the many last steps that had then always led him onwards, on and onwards. Ever onwards. The bullets in a Hamburg wall, 1923, lost Hamburg, the red uprising, the dead comrades in the camp, 1933, the human slaughterhouse, later and now, those screams, beaten to death, kicked to death, when they came for him, once, he'd thought: it's over now, and he'd thought nothing and had seen the skies, the dead comrades, Spanish skies, 1937, later and now, as blue and cloudy as anywhere else and everywhere and nowhere, hills like white elephants, blooded backs, bullets in walls, in flesh, *Fuhlsbüttel concentration camp*, yesterday and later and now.

And there in the camp he hadn't thought of him, had forgotten the great pirate of his childhood. Störtebeker. Divided. Severed. As he had placed the thin rope underneath his shirt. Ready to pull tight in an instant. Once more, to call out something no one would hear. To flee out of the darkness into the darkness.

And again, the light flickered in the cellar of the Lenin Library, and now he heard the distant thunder of the front, mixed as in the previous nights with the howling of the sirens.

He had barely slept for days. He had run off leaflets with his comrades. We're writing and writing and writing to the enemy. The printing presses rotated and he saw their sheets falling like pale autumn leaves out of the planes and onto the armies, *German soldiers, don't believe their lies! The Soviet Union is not your enemy!* in the language of his nation. No, his nation was *here*.

'We survived the hotel,' his friend Becher said, leaning on him.

'Shh... shh...' said Willi, as the sirens wailed above the cellars of the Lenin Library.

He wanted so much for Klaus to speak, for him to be heard, *sirens*, before he disappeared. Pulled himself together again.

To say that he knew victory was not lost in their time. To say he knew the legends that remained of him were so strong that the singers and the storytellers, *sirens*, would carry them down the centuries. *Had roamed – had become – had taken.*

'We won't get old.'

And Willi Bredel stood up and walked down the aisles and the shelves, walked along the books, walked between the walls of books, in which he had been seeking the truth about Störtebeker over the past months. The blood-blackened blocks.

He stood by the washbasin in the alcove. White enamel, the white flaking off. Tiny roads of rust. The tap dripped. How large and long these cellars were.

Where was the man who had sat in this alcove? He had never been alone down here. Willi Bredel heard a voice. Someone was whispering. Hoarse, hoarse and hurried. Or was it his own whisper? Whispered monologues. He had taken up whispering in the camp. He put his hand over his mouth. It was quiet now. Hands on his mouth. Hands on his mouth. He wanted to reach under his shirt. The thin rope must be gone. And he felt an urgent need to pee. He tugged his shirt out of his trousers and unbuttoned his fly. He groaned as his piss splashed into the basin. Peeing had been difficult since the camp. *Whipped, severed.* Drop by drop. And once he'd shaken it off and sat back down, a last remainder often shot into his underpants. Something must have got damaged. In the camp.

A mirror above the basin. So dull that he could barely see himself. Traces of limescale on the cracked glass. He turned on the tap and washed his face in the thin stream of water. Then he pressed his body, his abdomen, over the edge of the basin. He laid his hand on the glass, felt the cracks and the uneven surface, smooth and broken, wavy and cool, saw the outlines of his face, seeming to divide up into many faces, and when he moved his head his face contorted and was lost to either side. No, he saw nothing in the dull glass. And again, he heard the whispers, and this time he recognized the voice and he knew the poem: *I saw the Rothenburg Altar full of our faces. I saw it form an image of our time. I see gallows and crosses and blocks for heads rolling. In the midst of the image, blood breaks out. It bleeds in many places.*

'Becher, is that you?' he called into the mirror and turned around and called it into the room.

No, he had seen nothing in the mirror; he hated mirrors. They ought to take all mirrors down from the walls and smash them. Look out of the window! That's where the new man is. He leaned on the basin again, smelled his piss, turned the tap, water dripped onto his hand.

The new man. Willi Bredel laughed. *And blocks for heads rolling.* Hadn't it been Trotsky who first spoke of the new man? ('The Expressionists,' called Becher, shaking his fist, 'the Expressionists, not Trotsky!') No, no, that was a name they mustn't even think of. Even though the traitor had been liquidated in Mexico. Last year. 1940. The red battle. Divided. Severed. The new man had ripped apart his own flesh. The Comrade of Steel, bullets of steel... the hotel, Becher's nerves were shot. He remembered finding him in his room in those days, Becher, a needle in his arm, lying like a corpse on his bed. 'Hans, Hans, what on earth are you up to?'

And Becher, who came round again, the morphine red-black as poppies in his giant eyes, began quietly reciting Mayakovski: 'And he, the free man of whom I'm shouting, he will come, believe me, he will.'

Mayakovski, the great futurist... Willi Bredel would have liked to meet him, had always admired the power and strength of his language. He himself was just a simple working-class writer, had tried to learn from the great realists, 'don't put yourself down, Willi, old Valdimir' – he really said 'Valdimir' instead of 'Vladimir' – 'he chickened out, shot himself, if not even...' Becher moved his hand in the air, weighing up possibilities, and then made a gun out of his forefinger and thumb, and Bredel put a shocked finger on his lips, *silence or I'll shoot, comrades,* but Becher simply went on talking, 'but you're still here, Willi, carrying the proletarian literary flag of the revolution,' Becher seemed to be absolutely out of his mind, he pulled the syringe out of his arm and held it with the needle pointing at his friend Bredel, who took a silent step back. 'Religion is the opium of the people, but opium is the opium of the poet Becher!'

'Give that to me, Hans, now, be sensible!'

'Father Stalin loves his German comrades!'

'Hans, for God's sake...'

And Johannes Becher, whom Willi always called only 'Hans', talked about Feuerbach, 'the great philosopher and early communist', about glowing red streams burning their way down the centuries, he leapt to and fro in his crazed stories, talked about the brains of the dead, which the NKVD experimented with, which were connected up and could read thoughts.... talked and recited until he broke down in tears and fell asleep. Willi Bredel covered him up and went to the door. All the trials and tests, he thought as he closed the door behind him, there's no end to them, even here with our friends, but we believe, we believe in the new man, the new world...

'And more and more people turned against the un-Christian wealth and the inhumane tortures to which the poor were exposed,' wrote Willi Bredel at his desk in the cellar of the Lenin Library, as his friend Störtebeker wandered the seas in his time, when the powerful Hanseatic League ruled.

Störtebeker lived and worked with the fishermen. Saw and felt their lot. Saw how they were exploited. And Bredel created the powerful bailiff Wulflam, who was to stand for the exploiters in his novel. *I saw it form an image of our time*. Who punished arbitrarily, ordered hands be chopped off for the pettiest of crimes... And Störtebeker went to sea. Dreamed of the freedom of the seas. And Störtebeker became a helmsman. The intrigues of the powerful patrician Wulflam forced him to rise up. For even the sea was not free. Wulflam, a name he had found in the Lenin Library, in an old chronicle of the Hanseatic League, a wolf in lamb's clothing. 'It was a quiet night,' wrote Willi Bredel, 'the sea seemed to slumber,' while above him the city trembled and roared and the flak shot at the heavens, through which the enemy raged like the horsemen of the apocalypse...

He was briefly confused, and his Störtebeker saw the planes like giant steel gulls above the ship and in the midst of the clouds, and he held tight to the ship's wheel in fear.

Willi Bredel felt the pencil breaking in his hand. The roar of the flak had fallen silent. Willi Bredel tasted blood; his lips had split. His mouth was dry and his throat hurt when he swallowed. When he went to the alcove with the basin, the man who always sat there was back again. He wore a grey coat and a flat hat, which sometimes rested on his knees. Willi stopped a few yards away from him and said in Russian, 'Good evening, comrade!'

The man in grey merely nodded. Willi didn't know what to say. He had a pack of good French cigarettes in his inside pocket, but when he offered them to the man in grey, the man merely shook his head. Willi Bredel went back to his desk. Who did the man in grey remind him of, a gaunt man who sat there in his alcove, night after night... Who sometimes disappeared and then turned up again.

How many comrades had disappeared from the emigrants' hotel, as though given invisibility cloaks, props from dark fairy-tales. Willi Bredel listened for the clatter of the doors, footsteps in the corridors, knocks on doors, knocks on walls, he remembered the coded knocks with which the man in the next cell in Fuhlsbüttel had lent him courage, *be strong, comrade, think of the future, comrade, we will not lose courage and we will win out, comrade, believe in the future and in our people, comrade.* He had never seen him. Was he still in that camp? And Willi Bredel went back to his desk, and when he turned around again the chair in the alcove next to the basin was empty.

There had been a rumour going around for days that the German comrades would soon be leaving Moscow. Evacuation. For the Caucasus, apparently, evacuation to faraway Kazan. He wanted to stay here, he wanted to go to the front, he wanted to prove to the man in grey that he was prepared to die for communism and the Soviet Union. Just as his friend Störtebeker was prepared to die in battle. Yes, he was a German, and the Germans were setting fire to the land. Had burned his books too and almost burned him in the camp. Banned him. But he was a communist, stateless, *when I one day go home*, my state is utopia, is the Soviet Union, workers of the world, unite! And again he wrote. 'The storm whipped the sea.' You and I had no choice, he thought.

The pencil broke and again he wrote. How often had he flicked through the old chronicles over the past days and weeks? Deciphered reports on the privateer's deeds. Then too, they tried to unite them, the leagues, the tradesmen, the fishermen, the plebeians, the poor. And again he wrote.

'Daring rebels who rose up despite all dangers, revolted against those ruling by no right and no law, remained isolated in the North. They were secretly admired by the oppressed masses, but not actively supported. And these rebels, who rose up against an apparently invincible force, protecting themselves from persecution by the powerful of their time, were forced to be ruthless themselves.'

And Willi Bredel thought of all the dead, the

extinguished brains that his friend Becher saw over and over in his morphine visions, 'brains, Willi, they're stored everywhere in the cellars, the brains, Willi.'

In Spain they had executed anarchists who harmed the cause, had betrayed the cause. How many young men died on the fascists' side, drafted and stripped? He had seen the naked corpses in the Ebro. In one town – was it called Fuentes de Ebro? – his brigade had discovered a torture room in a monastery. He thought of the camp, Fuhlsbüttel, far away in the North but still there. In Spain they had captured a lieutenant and a priest, both apparently part of it, absolutions, screams, a unit of the Spanish republican army had taken charge of the two prisoners, Willi Bredel had turned away and heard the shots. He was a political commissar in the International Brigades, but the Spanish republican soldiers had lost friends and brothers.

'Klaus Störtebeker had taken up the sword, and in the battle against the cruelty of the wolves among men, he too knew no mercy.'

We must fight the Wulflams, isn't that right, my friend? But where are the Wulflams? Who are the Wulflams? Had they not made themselves into Wulflams? The great Comrade Wulflam, bullets of Wulflam. 'No, no, you mustn't even think that, Comrade Bredel!'

And Willi Bredel wrote and wrote, 'On his pirate ships, the rebellious spirit thrived, an impassioned hatred of patrician rule in the towns and of feudal lords in the countryside. But it was a dull, unfocused, anarchic spirit of rebellion, aimed only at destruction and damage to their enemies. They stole from the powerful what they too had merely stolen,' until his head sank onto the table and the papers.

And in his dream, deathly tired, so very tired, Willi

Bredel saw himself... oh, to sleep seven times seven years and wake up in a new world... and in his dream, Willi Bredel saw a mutant creature, a tall figure both wolf and lamb at once, which kept turning and turning and ripping its own flesh from its bones and fleeing in wild leaps from itself, stumbling through craters, through burning villages where it was singed by flames, past rivers flowing with naked corpses.

'Comrade Bredel, Störtebeker's anarchist tendencies are questionable and harm the cause of the Communist Party and the Communist International!'

'But comrades, Störtebeker is to some extent an early communist!'

'We expect you to distance yourself from Störtebeker, Comrade Bredel, we expect you to exert public criticism of his deviationism, Comrade Bredel!'

'But comrades, Störtebeker is part of the unified front against fascism, he's part of the Communist International!'

'Comrade Bredel, you were a political commissar in the International Brigades, you know that any deviation from the guiding lines of the Comintern and the Communist Party...'

'We made mistakes, comrades. We should have opposed the fascists with a united front, in Spain, comrades, and much earlier!'

'You're wrong, comrade, there was a united front against fascism in Spain! Our glorious International Brigades. Do you want to besmirch the legacy of Comrade Thälmann, Comrade Bredel, by questioning our struggle in the hard years?'

'But comrades, Comrade Thälmann was like a father to me! He sat at our table when I was young, and once he even told the story of Comrade Störtebeker!'

'We must block out personal sentimentalities, Comrade Bredel. The party is always right. And your Störtebeker, did he not make a pact with the enemy, did he not shake the hands of the patricians?'

'But comrades, that was just a ruse! Our Comrade of Steel did the same...'

'Comrade Bredel, how dare you speak so outrageously about the Great General, about our beloved Comrade Stalin!'

'But comrades, I love him too! But we must not send Comrade Störtebeker into exile or death too. The enemy is at the gates, comrades!'

And Willi Bredel woke up and felt the cold. He was wrapped in a blanket and the snow dazzled him. For a moment he didn't know where he was – had they sent him to Siberia, what had he done to be sent into exile? – but had the *what* ever mattered, hadn't he exerted self-criticism, 'I admit to my mistakes, comrades,' he had shown doubt in the Comrade of Steel, had questioned him, doubted – was he on one of those islands of ice? – the camp, the House of the Dead, the island of Sakhalin on which the prisoners dwelled, icy cold, Napoleon in the snow – and then he heard the front. Dull thuds, thunder of cannons, *the storm whipped the sea*, and soon he'd stopped flinching when grenades exploded nearby, he was Störtebeker standing calmly at the wheel, no fear – we can bear thunder and lightning and storm, can't we, my friend, we can change the thunder and lightning of history, can't we, comrade? – and Bredel thought of his friend Becher, who told him about Feuerbach and discussed Marx's famous theses in quiet whispers by night in the hotel, *not to interpret, but to change!* If the enemy wins out, that is the end of history.

He sat, wrapped in a blanket, in the door of a dugout,

holding his cold tobacco pipe in his hand and looking at the dark red sky of the front.

Someone shook him. Two young soldiers. They had to go forward to the Germans, lay wires, install loudspeakers, and then back through the snow. The snow was never bloody for long; it snowed almost without pause.

They had dropped leaflets like snowflakes, onto the Germans advancing upon Moscow, thousands and thousands, which the wind had sometimes driven back into the city.

But that had been in autumn.

Willi Bredel blinked into the white; he could barely see his fellow soldiers in their snow-camouflage suits. And he hoped the Germans couldn't spot them either from behind their lines. Evening came, and the red of the short winter dusk mingled with the eternal red of the war sky, streams of fire in the darkness, sometimes he didn't know exactly where he was, Voronezh, Moscow, somewhere outside Stalingrad, he barely slept now, felt like he hadn't slept properly since 1936. His chest often ached. What was it his friend Becher had said? 'Hearts made of paper.'

He watched the two young soldiers attaching the loudspeaker to a wall, the remains of a farmstead; more than once, a hand had protruded from the snow on their paths between the fronts. If it was a German hand, a German uniform poking through the snow in front of them, stiff as a long piece of wood, the two of them had often made a joke, 'Your last *Sieg Heil*, soldier,' and Störtebeker laughed his bitter laugh. He had re-written the beginning of his novel, one evening before, in the brief calm of the dugout.

'What are you writing, comrade?'

'A story about a German buccaneer.'

'We've got enough German buccaneers out there.' The young soldier pointed at the door of the dugout. A few of the men standing around laughed. Young men, unshaven, smoking, some still with soft boys' moustaches. But Willi Bredel didn't let them break his stride; he had grown up as a worker's son among workers and he had lived to tell the tale of a war in Spain. He smiled at the young men and filled his pipe.

'Störtebeker was a revolutionary, comrades, a young fighter, full of strength, like you. Full of dreams, like you. And he lived in a time of great struggles, five hundred years ago now, when the fishermen and tradesmen and workers joined forces, but many lacked courage. The enemy seemed too powerful.'

The men were now quiet and had gathered around Willi Bredel, who was sitting by one of the potbellied stoves in which a tiny pile of embers still glowed – stories and warmth. 'And do you know, comrades, why they called him Störtebeker? It was just a... code name.' He spoke Russian to the young soldiers, but he pronounced the pirate's name in German. 'Stör-te-be-ker. It means something like *Drink the beaker...*' He searched for the Russian words; like most of the Germans in Comintern, he had started learning Russian early on, the language of the revolution. 'That means something like *Knock it back, the full mug!*'

He formed a giant beer mug in the air and lifted it jerkily to his lips. The young soldiers laughed. And Willi Bredel took his silver hipflask with the red star out of the inside pocket of his field coat and passed it to the soldiers standing around him.

'It's beautiful,' said one very young man, and ran his finger very carefully over the silver metal and the red star. He was wearing an army shapka stuffed with newspaper because it was too big for him. Willi Bredel had seen the paper when he nervously took it off and put it on again when grenades hit nearby, some time in the evening or in the day, and he saw it again when the shapka lay in the snow, some time in the evening, some time in the day, the crumpled newspaper dark and stained.

And Willi Bredel went on with the story of Störtebeker, the freebooter, the storm-rider, his adventures on land and at sea, and the soldiers listened. Soon they'd be back on the field, in the cold, in the fire, in the darkness, in the fear, in the never-ending battle.

'What did you just write?' one of them asked.

'I killed a friend of Störtebeker's,' said Bredel, drawing on his pipe, which he hadn't lit yet; he was frugal with his good tobacco.

The soldiers grew restless. The death of a friend – that they knew.

And Willi Bredel was sorry he had to talk about it now. The next deployment was fast approaching.

'I'm often ashamed to be German, now,' Willi Bredel said.

In the barracks, in the dugout, it was silent. Willi Bredel heard the quiet crackle of the embers in the stove. 'No, no,' he said as the soldiers tried to contradict him, saying he wasn't one of *those* Germans, he was a communist, a comrade.

'I believe in the new Germany, comrades, in the land of Marx and Engels and Thälmann. But after all I've seen in the past weeks and months...' he fell silent. Sucked on his cold pipe. 'Störtebeker's friend was an old Jew. And I burned him. In here.' He held up the large notebook from his lap, containing many of his folded Moscow manuscript pages. 'Burned alive,' he said then, slightly quieter. And the soldiers understood; some of them nodded.

And Willi Bredel squatted behind the soot-blackened wall that had once been part of the farmstead and saw the two young soldiers setting up the loudspeakers for his speeches. He wanted to ask them where they were exactly, surely not in Voronezh any more, probably somewhere outside Stalingrad, but then he didn't and he looked out across the wide steppes of snow, behind which the Germans were sitting somewhere, not far away.

'*Für unser Volk und Vaterland!* Against Hitler and his war! For immediate peace! For the rescue of the German people! German soldiers, come to us! Don't believe your officers' lies! Don't believe Hitler's lies. The Soviet Union is not your enemy! Listen to your conscience! Stop being accomplices to the terrible crimes! Come to a world of peace between our nations! We will take you in, German soldiers, we are waiting for you, German soldiers, there's no need to be afraid if you come to us! The glorious Soviet power is strong but it is also just! Together, we shall shape the new world after Hitler! Look to your homeland, German soldiers – the fire your lying leaders have brought here is now burning around your families! Let us extinguish it together!'

And Willi Bredel, the working-class writer from Hamburg, *oh, lost Hamburg, when I one day come home*, took his shapka off his head and turned away from the microphone and coughed into his hat. How many of them over there might come from Hamburg? Once, he hadn't been careful enough and his cough had rolled like thunder across the crater-ridden snowscape. And he could imagine the officers over there laughing at him. While they shot at him.

No, he had never laughed when the two young soldiers

made their jokes about the frozen German arms, the frozen German army emerging from the snow. Too many young German men who had been blinded, seduced, too many young hands that would never be able to clear the rubble. No, there wasn't much to laugh about in this cold time. Perhaps a bitter laugh. Which he then so often wrote into the lines of his Störtebeker.

'And how did he die?' the curious young soldier with the newspaper-stuffed hat had asked.

'I told you, they burned him.'

'No, Comrade Author, not the old Jew. Your Störtebeker, the pirate comrade.'

And Willi Bredel told the soldiers how the freebooter had walked upright to the scaffold where the executioner was waiting for him with his sword.

'He only fell into their hands through deception and betrayal. He had forged a pact with the patricians, but it was a pact with the devil.'

The soldiers nodded. They lived in a time of betrayal and fear of denunciation. And Willi Bredel remembered the great pact with which the Comrade of Steel, in whom they nonetheless believed and would forever believe, had surprised them all, had scared them. He'd been in Spain at the time (or was he on his way back from Spain by then? the long march of the International Brigades, oh, lost brigades), the fight against fascism, *no pasarán!* and then that had happened – the world seemed to be coming apart at the seams, had already come apart. The wise comrade knows what he's doing, they had consoled each other, the wise comrade is playing chess with the devil. Wulflam, Wulflam, the wolf is creeping in, and it crept by night through the corridors of the hotel where the German comrades lived, and the rooms emptied out. And the last of the comrades sat together and sang the

Internationale. *The earth belongs to us, the workers... not the noisome birds of prey.*

'And one of the patricians, one of the rich and powerful men and warlords, Alderman Miles, mocked him and asked if he felt sorrow that he must die.'

Willi Bredel huddled behind the wall. The wail of the grenades. Snow fell and his face was clammy and wet, and he felt the hipflask in his inside pocket, a gift from a long-lost friend, one last sip, good cognac, the wail of the grenades. But they struck far away. He never heard the rifle shots. Sometimes he saw the snipers' bullets whisking up fountains of snow. So close. And he reached for the microphone, for the broadcaster, and his voice echoed through the morning's expanse.

'"My own death causes me no sorrow," answered Comrade Störtebeker, "for I have lived, and I have fought, and I have often enough kicked you where it hurts!"'

The young soldiers laughed, some had gripped each other's shoulders and were looking at each other as they laughed, their unshaven, dirty and haggard faces no longer marked by the furrows of fear and concern and exhaustion, no, furrows of laughter, and Willi Bredel too laughed and tapped at the air with the stem of his cold pipe. 'And I assure you, comrades, he really did kick them often and hard enough where it hurts!'

A snowstorm had set in and they had retreated to a crater behind the wall, had covered themselves with the padded white tarpaulins they always took along, lay tightly packed. They couldn't stay here all too long, just a brief rest and to wait until the worst was over. And now Willi Bredel knew where he was – somewhere ahead of them, behind them, lay Stalingrad.

'And then the powerful patrician, still wanting to torment Störtebeker, asked whether he did not regret the death of his companions. For Störtebeker's crewmates were lined up before the scaffold. For they too were to be executed. Yes, said Störtebeker, his companions, they should not die, for he was dying for them. And he looked right in the eye of the powerful patrician who mocked him so.'

Some of the soldiers had sat down on the floor of the barracks, the dugout, in front of Willi Bredel. Someone passed him the silver hipflask with the red star and Willi Bredel shook it; there seemed to be a little sip left in the metal flask, and he put it to his lips and drank. 'Go on with the story, Comrade Störtebeker.'

And later, back in Moscow, in the cellar of the Lenin Library, he tried to remember how he'd survived it all. He had taken a train back from the front. They needed him again in Moscow. The fascists were on the retreat – they didn't like to use the term National Socialists, the socialists were the heritage and the future – the fascists were on the retreat, like Napoleon before them in the snow.

He had taken a train to the front as well – how many months ago? Years and decades. Moscow, Voronezh, Stalingrad. Or had he been on a plane? His Moscow apartment was empty, the windows broken, the neighbouring buildings burned out. Thank goodness he carried the manuscript in the inside pocket of his field coat. When he opened the window and stuck his head into the cold wind, he saw the steaming, stomping locomotives, the cars camouflaged with white tarpaulins in the snowy wastes they were crossing, and Willi Bredel blinked into the white.

And he thought of the soldiers who had marched towards Stalingrad. How they had laughed at first, and how they then listened in awe as he told them about

Störtebeker's death. 'And when the blade severed his head from his shoulders, his tall body rose to its feet and walked past his companions, waiting in a line for their death by the scaffold. Just as Störtebeker had told the powerful Alderman Miles he would do. For he had promised him in jest to spare every one of his companions whom he walked past after his execution. And so Störtebeker, legend has it, walked with a slow sway, bleeding but upright, past his companions, for his death was not to be in vain.'

'Still working on th-that Stör-te-te-be-ker, comrade?' Startled, Willi Bredel lifted his head from the desk, where he had been bent over the fanned-out pages. Behind him, in the semi-darkness of the huge cellar vault of Moscow's Lenin Library, stood a thin man, holding his flat hat in front of his chest in both hands. At first, Willi Bredel thought the man in grey was back, the one who had always sat in the alcove with the washbasin, but then he recognized his unexpected guest and remembered his nervous stutter, which only broke off when he got into his agitprop stride.

'Good evening, Comrade Kurella,' he said and stood up. 'I thought you were somewhere in the Caucasus.'

'I'm on my w-w-way there, Com-Comrade Bredel. You kn-know your st-stuff.'

'So do you,' said Willi Bredel, nodding briefly at the manuscript pages on the desk. Only a few people knew that he was wrestling with the Störtebeker material down here. He had thought a few times about reading from the manuscript, for German prisoners-of-war, to whom he usually read from his concentration camp novel, or on Radio Moskau. It was almost finished actually, his Störtebeker novel, but he was still looking for a title, *The Equal Sharers*, that was the meaning of the

214

Likedeelers to whom Störtebeker belonged, or perhaps simply *Störtebeker* or *The Struggle for Rights* or *Come Back, Störtebeker* or *Comrade Störtebeker's Great Struggle*, the last few revisions, but he kept feeling unhappy with it, he wanted Störtebeker to strike his cutlass into the here and now. He had thought a few times about somehow linking his Stalingrad story, which he had started writing ('An ocean of frozen rubble, a city now made up only of cellars and the dead, ghosts in ragged uniforms creeping through the horror...'), somehow tying it in with the historical material about the Likedeelers, but he was a working-class writer and not James Joyce, and he stared at the desk strewn with papers, perplexed.

'You d-d-do kn-know, comrade, that your Stör-te-te-be-ker probably ne-never existed, that a Buccaneer Störtebek-Störtebeker is just an old le-legend.'

'Perhaps, Comrade Kurella, but what do we need more in these times than legends?'

'I'm sure you're r-right, if they serve our c-cause.'

They walked slowly side by side along the endless aisles of high shelves, turned here and there, strolled, paused by several particularly impressive spines, and Willi Bredel, who only came up to the tall thin man's shoulder, wondered what Kurella might want from him. They had both lived in the hotel in the mid-thirties and as the rooms began to empty out, Kurella's brother, who lived with him in the hotel, had disappeared like so many German communists, clad in invisibility cloaks from old fairy-tales. But Kurella didn't disappear. He had met Lenin as a young man, everyone knew that, and his stutter came from the frontlines of the first great war. From the beginning of the great war that never ended. In the empty rooms, they whispered that Kurella had denounced his own brother. Bredel had never believed that.

215

'How did Gorky put it?' Bredel said, looking at the thin face and the already silvery, thinning hair of Comrade Kurella, who was standing in front of a shelf and stroking one of the gold-printed spines with his long index finger. 'Not just the gun must fight for our cause...'

'N-n-not just the gun, but also the word,' Kurella completed Bredel's sentence and turned to him. 'That's exactly wh-why I'm here, comrade.'

Then Kurella took one of his famous loaded pauses, linked arms with Bredel, for which he had to lean over slightly, and then the two comrades strolled arm in arm, swaying a little due to their very different heights, along the endless shelved aisles of the Lenin Library.

'I must confess, comrade,' said Willi Bredel, 'that I was wrong...'

'Wrong, Com-Comrade Bredel? Are you exer-exercising self-criticism?'

'No, no, comrade. But I believe it was Renn, our outstanding Spain veteran Ludwig Renn, who was the source of that quote about guns and words...'

'Yes, Com-Comrade Bredel, b-but he was re-remarking on a famous essay by Gorky.'

'Possibly, comrade, but I believe that Gorky, before he died...'

And so they debated, as they walked on, passing the alcove with the dull mirror above the washbasin – it had a large crack, the mirrors had cracked in all of Moscow – and Bredel asked Comrade Kurella, knowing his influence and the apparent wealth of information at his disposal about what lay in darkness for himself, about the writer Babel, who had lived in Moscow for a long time. Willi Bredel had read Babel's *Red Cavalry* years ago.

Bredel knew Gorky had protected the writer Babel

when he was attacked because he tried to depict the reality of the civil war, the long-over and never-over... Ach, reality... Bredel was suddenly very tired and it seemed to him as if they had been walking for hours along the aisles of books and paper. How often had he asked himself, as he sketched out his Ebro stories in Spain, how much he could describe the fascists' brutality and their own brutality in the fight against brutality. Just as he had read in Babel's work, he too wished to write about the fights and the living and the dead, crystal clear so that every reader would weep over the war and every war.

Sometimes he no longer knew whether he lied and lied or wrote fairy-tales and made dark fairy-tales into bright ones, or whether he was helping to lay the ground for the new time, as he hoped he was.

'Babel?' Kurella was not stuttering now. 'Like the Tower of Babel.'

He said nothing more about the writer Babel, who had disappeared like the bees in one of his stories that Willi Bredel remembered, beehives, smoked out. But who will pollinate the bees, then? Willi Bredel thought. Us?

But they lived in a time that needed Störtebekers. And no sentimentalities, comrades! Man's twilight may fall if fascism is not rooted out! But that does sound rather expressionist, and Comrade Kurella distanced himself very clearly from expressionism in his theoretical writings.

His friend Becher, whom he had not seen for a long time, was afraid of Kurella. *Not seen for a long time* was never a good thing in those days that never ended. Years, decades.

Becher, a needle in his arm, stretched out on the bed of his room in the hotel, his eyes widened and black-red as poppies – what had he once said about Kurella? Willi Bredel thought back. 'He has no shadow, that man, take a close look, comrade, when he creeps along the corridors, there's no shadow behind that man.'

If only that were true, Hans. They all had shadows, shadows over shadows, attached to them, dragging after them, small and large ones, dark ones and grey ones and sometimes stained red, 'Yes, you're right, Bredel, but him, he hasn't got one, take a close look.' His friend Becher, stretched out on the bed, whispered monologues, hoarse whispering, eyes widened and large as poppies.

And later, long after Kurella had left the cellar of the Moscow Lenin Library, Willi Bredel stood in front of the dull cracked mirror, leaned on the washbasin, turned on the tap and drank. The water ran cool over his hand and he wet his forehead.

'When I come back,' Kurella had told him, 'I have plans, and I need you for them, you and your Störtebeker.'

'Where will you come back to?' Bredel had asked Kurella, 'and when will you come back?' Coming back was a tricky thing to do in those days.

'To the new Germany, Comrade Bredel, the new Germany.'

They stood on the narrow balcony beneath the dome of the great metro station, the walls of marble, the crystal chandeliers before them. Bredel felt tiny on that balcony, accessed through a door between two shelves at the end of an aisle, to which Kurella had strode purposefully. Willi Bredel handed him the box of French cigarettes, but Kurella turned them down.

'Look at this wealth, comrade, created by the people, for the people.'

And below them, the first metro trains were running again, people standing on the platforms with chandeliers illuminating them, crystal dazzling them when the lights of the trains struck it. 'Yes,' said Bredel, 'the world should see what socialism can achieve,' and he remembered the months when the bombs were falling, when the people stood packed like sardines down here. If only Stalingrad had had a metro system.

'I want to build a new school,' said Kurella, leaning on the balustrade, and Bredel was suddenly scared the other man might stumble and fall and he'd get the blame.

'I want to found a school where we propagate the new literature, where working-class children become writers, and that's what I need you for, Comrade Bredel!'

'Like the Gorky Institute on Tverskoy Boulevard?' Bredel asked.

'Yes, Comrade Bredel, a brother institute in the new Germany.'

'We'll have to build it first, that new Germany.'

'You don't doubt, do you, Comrade Bredel?'

'No, we have never doubted,' said Bredel.

And standing in front of the cracked, dull mirror, leaning on the washbasin, the empty hipflask with the red star embossed onto silver in his inside pocket, Willi Bredel once again saw the flash of the crystals in the giant chandeliers, saw the cathedral-like metro station, heard Comrade Kurella, 'Rewrite it for the youth, your Störtebeker novel, an uplifting book for the youth of our new Germany,' remembered his friend Becher showing him a book in the hotel, a fairy-tale from the days of German Romanticism, illustrated by the expressionist Kirchner, there he was, Kurella, the man in grey, gaunt and wearing a flat working-man's cap, harried and driven – 'I want to build a school!' – Bredel had looked at that

219

book for a long time at night, first published 1814, 'The events of the world... tore me apart, in many ways, on many days,' – where are you, Störtebeker, political commissar? – 'We have never doubted,' and in the flash of the crystals he saw a metro train carrying all the lost comrades, looking mutely up at them as they leaned on the balustrade, and Willi Bredel saw himself on the train, Moscow–Stalingrad–Moscow – how long ago was that now? – never and forever, he was startled at first because he believed for a moment he had seen himself among the lost, but he had been tortured by Nazis, he had survived the camp and the escape, *when I one day come home*, 'but how can that be, comrades, that other comrades would betray...' 'You mustn't even think that, Willi!' *divided, severed*, and he was back with the German comrades in the train compartment while outside the snowy wastes, human wastes, rubble wastes flew by, people fleeing the horrors, groups of people, dark dots in the snow, with wagons, on foot, and Bredel read from his novel *Die Väter*, which had been published in the journal *Internationale Literatur*, 'Read, Comrade Bredel,' called Comrade Ulbricht, political commissar, leading propagandist, 'Read something amusing!' and Bredel stared into the dull mirror, coded knocks, laid one hand on the glass, he was tired, so infinitely tired – 'Infinity, comrades? We don't discuss those problems here!' – knocks, a man in his cell, beaten and tormented, people in their cells, beaten and tormented, and Willi Bredel, working-class writer from Hamburg, saw Becher's altar on the face of the dull mirror in the cellar of the Moscow Lenin Library, *From the midst of the image, blood breaks out*, he rested his forehead on the dull and wavy looking-glass, Becher's morphine fantasias, he sees satellite towns, large factories with flames shooting out of their chimneys, sees the breaking and falling of concrete, plinths without statues, dragged down, toppled, *had roamed – had become – had taken*, hears the knocks behind the mirror, 'How will we one day be remembered,' sees and hears, full of horror – 'I let the comrade deceive me' – himself denying an old comrade from the Spanish war – is this the new Germany we dreamed up? – clutches his aching chest, over and over, *hearts made of paper*, sees wars and revolutions and wars, toppled statues, falling walls, 'Then that's the end of history,' sparkling minarets and extinguishing red stars, people starving and fleeing, *had roamed, had taken*, sees himself in the train compartment with his comrades, 'shot', in the new school in the new Germany, in the Gorky Institute, 'an uplifting novel for the youth, comrade, something like your humorous novel about working-class Hamburg!' *oh, lost Hamburg*, Carl Benten, you permanently drunk troublemaker!, *'Ick bin für dee Niggers!'* – *Die Väter, Die Söhne, Die Enkel*, did I write all that? – 'Damnit, what the hell are we doing in Africa! Why are the poor negroes getting slaughtered? Because the lords of iron and steel crave even fatter profits. Who gets rich on the treasures of Africa's soil? Do we? No, it's the insatiable industrialists,' badamm, badamm, badamm, over the railway sleepers of the new time, 'Something amusing, comrade! We know what imperialism is like, we're not in re-education camp here!' riding the waves of the new time as Störtebeker, too many Wulflams! calls the ancient captain, greed, falsity and cruelty rule the world, and Willi Bredel tore himself away from the images, which he saw like in a fever in the dull mirror, and staggered exhausted back to the desk, on which the pages of his manuscript waited for him, always blank and always new.

Fitzcarraldo Editions
8-12 Creekside
London, SE8 3DX
United Kingdom

Copyright © Clemens Meyer, 2017
Originally published in Germany by S. Fischer Verlag in 2017
Translation copyright © Katy Derbyshire, 2020
This edition first published in Great Britain by
Fitzcarraldo Editions in 2020

The right of Clemens Meyer to be identified as the author
of this work has been asserted in accordance with
Section 77 of the Copyright, Designs and Patents Act 1988.

ISBN 978-1-913097-13-4

Design by Ray O'Meara
Typeset in Fitzcarraldo
Printed and bound by TJ International

All rights reserved. No part of this publication may be
reproduced, stored in a retrieval system or transmitted
in any form or by any means, electronic, mechanical,
photocopying, recording or otherwise, without prior
permission in writing from Fitzcarraldo Editions.

The translation of this work was supported by
a grant from the Goethe-Institut London

Fitzcarraldo Editions